ASSUMPTION

Yellow leaves and
bright orange afternoons.
Mornings
that carry the bite of fall and air
so clean and clear
that we leap into the day.
A friendship time.

Early September!

Early September

An Anthology of Short Stories

Edited by
James A. MacNeill

NELSON CANADA LIMITED

Pupil's Edition ISBN 0-17-600749-0
Teacher's Edition ISBN 0-17-601427-6

Printed and bound in Canada

13   14   15   16   17   BP 432109

Table of Contents

Clash and Conflict

Struggle is life. Muscles become stronger as a runner struggles against time to break the record in a 100-m sprint. Reactions become quicker as an astronaut trains for the journey into space. The instinct to survive becomes keener when a jungle explorer is pitted against the powers of the rain forest. The clash and conflict of our existence hold our deepest interest. Struggle is the salt of life.

In this section we see two main types of conflict. INTERNAL CONFLICT involves a struggle of the mind within and against itself, the great striving of the mind to find peace or balance. EXTERNAL CONFLICT involves characters battling against nature or opposing one another. The guilty conscience is an example of internal conflict. A character fighting a raging blizzard, or two rivals competing for the same prize, are examples of external conflict.

Often it is not so much the conflict but the outcome that is important in a short story. How the struggle is resolved tells us whether the ordeal was beneficial or destructive to the character.

The stories in this unit show people in conflict and show how they react under pressure. If we read carefully, we can find out a great deal about the fictional characters and perhaps something about ourselves. As you read, try asking, "What would I do in that situation?" Your answer might give you a new insight into yourself.

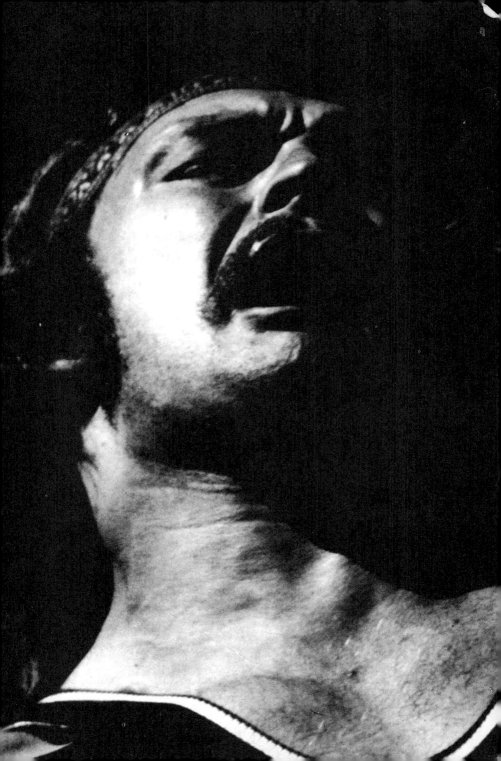

The Old Demon

Pearl S. Buck

"You old demon!" she said severely. Let the river god hear it if he liked. He was evil, that he was — so to threaten flood when there had been all this other trouble.

Old Mrs. Wang knew of course that there was a war. Everybody had known for a long time that there was war going on and that Japanese were killing Chinese. But still it was not real and no more than hearsay since none of the Wangs had been killed. The village of Three Mile Wangs on the flat banks of the Yellow River, which was old Mrs. Wang's clan village, had never even seen a Japanese. This was how they came to be talking about Japanese at all.

It was evening and early summer, and after her supper Mrs. Wang had climbed the dike steps, as she did every day, to see how high the river had risen. She was much more afraid of the river than of the Japanese. She knew what the river would do. And one by one the villagers had followed her up the dike, and now they stood staring down at the malicious yellow water, curling along like a lot of snakes, and biting at the high dike banks.

"I never saw it as high as this so early," Mrs. Wang said. She sat down on a bamboo stool that her grandson, Little Pig, had brought for her, and spat into the water.

"It's worse than the Japanese, this old devil of a river," Little Pig said recklessly.

"Fool!" Mrs. Wang said quickly. "The river god will hear you. Talk about something else."

So they had gone on talking about the Japanese. . . . How, for instance, asked Wang, the baker, who was old Mrs. Wang's nephew twice removed, would they know the Japanese when they saw them?

Mrs. Wang at this point said positively, "You'll know them. I once saw a foreigner. He was taller than the eaves of my house and he had mud-colored hair and eyes the color of a fish's eyes. Anyone who does not look like us — that is a Japanese."

Everybody listened to her since she was the oldest woman in the village and whatever she said settled something.

Then Little Pig spoke up in his disconcerting way. "You can't see them, Grandmother. They hide up in the sky in airplanes."

Mrs. Wang did not answer immediately. Once she would have said positively, "I shall not believe in an airplane until I see it." But so many things had been true which she had not believed—the Empress, for instance, whom she had not believed dead, was dead. The republic, again, she had not believed in because she did not know what it was. She still did not know, but they had said for a long time there had been one. So now she merely stared quietly about the dike where they all sat around her. It was very pleasant and cool, and she felt nothing mattered if the river did not rise to flood.

"I don't believe in the Japanese," she said flatly.

They laughed at her a little, but no one spoke. Someone lit her pipe — it was Little Pig's wife, who was her favorite, and she smoked it.

"Sing, Little Pig!" someone called.

So Little Pig began to sing an old song in a high quavering voice, and old Mrs. Wang listened and forgot the Japanese. The evening was beautiful, the sky so clear and still that the willows overhanging the dike were reflected even in the muddy water. Everything was at peace. The thirty-odd houses which made up the village straggled along beneath them. Nothing could break this peace. After all, the Japanese were only human beings.

"I doubt those airplanes," she said mildly to Little Pig when he stopped singing.

But without answering her, he went on to another song.

Year in and year out she had spent the summer evenings like this on the dike. The first time she was seventeen and a bride, and her husband had shouted to her to come out of the house and up the dike, and she had come, blushing and twisting her hands together, to hide among the women while the men roared at her and made jokes about her. All the same, they had liked her. "A pretty piece of meat in your bowl," they had said to her husband. "Feet a trifle big," he had answered deprecatingly. But she could see he was pleased, and so gradually her shyness went away.

He, poor man, had been drowned in a flood when he was still young. And it had taken her years to get him prayed out of Buddhist purgatory. Finally she had grown tired of it, what with the child and the land all on her back, and so when the priest said coaxingly, "Another ten pieces of silver and he'll be out entirely," she asked, "What's he got in there yet?"

"Only his right hand," the priest said, encouraging her.

Well, then, her patience broke. Ten dollars! It would feed them for the winter. Besides, she had had to hire labor for her share of repairing the dike, too, so there would be no more floods.

"If it's only one hand, he can pull himself out," she said firmly.

She often wondered if he had, poor silly fellow. As like as not, she had often thought gloomily in the night, he was still lying there, waiting for her to do something about it. That was the sort of man he was. Well, someday, perhaps, when Little Pig's wife had had the first baby safely and she had a little extra, she might go back to finish him out of purgatory. There was no real hurry, though. . . .

"Grandmother, you must go in," Little Pig's wife's soft voice said. "There is a mist rising from the river now that the sun is gone."

"Yes, I suppose I must," old Mrs. Wang agreed. She gazed at the river a moment. That river — it was full of good and evil together. It would water the fields when it was curbed and checked, but then if an inch were allowed in, it crashed through like a roaring dragon. That was how her husband had been swept away — careless, he was, about his bit of the dike. He was always going to mend it, always going to pile more earth on top of it, and then in a night the river rose and broke through. He had run out of the house, and she had climbed on the roof with the child and had saved herself and it while he was drowned. Well, they had pushed the river back again behind its dikes, and it had stayed there this time. Every day she herself walked up and down the length of the dike for which the village was responsible and examined it. The men laughed and said, "If anything is wrong with the dikes, Granny will tell us."

It had never occurred to any of them to move the village away from the river. The Wangs had lived there for generations, and some had always escaped the floods and had fought the river more fiercely than ever afterward.

Little Pig suddenly stopped singing.

"The moon is coming up!" he cried. "That's not good. Airplanes come out on moonlight nights."

"Where do you learn all this about airplanes?" old Mrs. Wang exclaimed. "It is tiresome to me," she added, so severely that no one spoke. In this silence, leaning upon the arm of Little Pig's wife, she descended slowly the earthen steps which led down into the village, using her long pipe in the other hand as a walking stick. Behind her the villagers came down, one by one, to bed. No one moved before she did, but none stayed long after her. And in her own bed at last, behind the blue cotton mosquito curtains which Little Pig's wife fastened securely, she fell peacefully asleep. She had lain awake a little while thinking about the Japanese and wondering why they wanted to fight. Only very coarse persons wanted wars. In her mind she saw large coarse persons. If they came one must wheedle them, she thought, invite them to drink tea, and explain to them, reasonably—only why should they come to a peaceful farming village . . . ?

So she was not in the least prepared for Little Pig's wife screaming at her that the Japanese had come. She sat up in bed muttering. "The tea bowls — the tea — "

"Grandmother, there's no time!" Little Pig's wife screamed. "They're here — they're here!"

"Where?" old Mrs. Wang cried, now awake.

"In the sky!" Little Pig's wife wailed.

They had all run out at that, into the clear early dawn, and gazed up. There, like wild geese flying in autumn, were great birdlike shapes.

"But what are they?" old Mrs. Wang cried.

And then, like a silver egg dropping, something drifted straight down and fell at the far end of the village in a field. A fountain of earth flew up, and they all ran to see it. There was a hole thirty feet across, as big as a pond. They were so astonished they could not speak, and then, before anyone could say anything, another and another egg began to fall and everybody was running, running. . . .

Everybody, that is, but Mrs. Wang. When Little Pig's wife seized her hand to drag her along, old Mrs. Wang pulled away and sat down against the bank of the dike.

"I can't run," she remarked. "I haven't run in seventy years, since before my feet were bound. You go on. Where's Little Pig?" She looked around. Little Pig was already gone. "Like his grandfather," she remarked, "always the first to run."

But Little Pig's wife would not leave her, not, that is, until old Mrs. Wang reminded her that it was her duty.

"If Little Pig is dead," she said, "then it is necessary that his son be born alive." And when the girl still hesitated, she struck at her gently with her pipe. "Go on — go on," she exclaimed.

So unwillingly, because now they could scarcely hear each other speak for the roar of the dipping planes, Little Pig's wife went on with the others.

By now, although only a few minutes had passed, the village was in ruins and the straw roofs and wooden beams were blazing. Everybody was gone. As they passed they had shrieked at old Mrs. Wang to come on, and she had called back pleasantly: "I'm coming—I'm coming!"

But she did not go. She sat quite alone watching now what was an extraordinary spectacle. For soon other planes came, from where she did not know, but they attacked the first ones. The sun came up over the fields of ripening wheat, and in the clear summery air the planes wheeled and darted and spat at each other. When this was over, she thought, she would go back into the village and see if anything was left. Here and there a wall stood, supporting a roof. She could not see her own house from here. But she was not unused to war. Once bandits had looted their village, and houses had been burned then, too. Well, now it had happened again. Burning houses one could see often, but not this darting silvery shining battle in the air. She understood none of it—not what those things were, nor how they stayed up in the sky. She simply sat, growing hungry, and watching.

"I'd like to see one close," she said aloud. And at that moment, as though in answer, one of them pointed suddenly downward, and, wheeling and twisting as though it were wounded, it fell head down in a field which Little Pig had plowed only yesterday for soybeans. And in an instant the sky was empty again and there was only this wounded thing on the ground and herself.

She hoisted herself carefully from the earth. At her age she need be afraid of nothing. She could, she decided, go and see what it was. So leaning on her bamboo pipe, she made her way slowly across the fields. Behind her in the sudden stillness two or three village dogs appeared and followed, creeping close to her in their terror. When they drew near to the fallen plane, they barked furiously. Then she hit them with her pipe.

"Be quiet," she scolded, "there's already been noise enough to split my ears!"

She tapped the airplane.

"Metal," she told the dogs. "Silver, doubtless," she added. Melted up, it would make them all rich.

She walked around it, examining it closely. What made it fly? It seemed dead. Nothing moved or made a sound within it. Then, coming to the side to which it tipped, she saw a young man in it, slumped into a heap in a little seat. The dogs growled, but she struck at them again and they fell back.

"Are you dead?" she inquired politely.

The young man moved a little at her voice, but did not speak. She drew nearer and peered into the hole in which he sat. His side was bleeding.

"Wounded!" she exclaimed. She took his wrist. It was warm, but inert, and when she let it go, it dropped against the side of the hole. She stared at him. He had black hair and a dark skin like a Chinese and still he did not look like a Chinese.

"He must be a Southerner," she thought. Well, the chief thing was, he was alive.

"You had better come out," she remarked. "I'll put some herb plaster on your side."

The young man muttered something dully.

"What did you say?" she asked. But he did not say it again.

"I am still quite strong," she decided after a moment. So she reached in and seized him about the waist and pulled him out slowly, panting a good deal. Fortunately he was rather a little fellow and very light.

When she had him on the ground, he seemed to find his feet; and he stood shakily and clung to her, and she held him up.

"Now if you can walk to my house," she said, "I'll see if it is there."

Then he said something, quite clearly. She listened and could not understand a word of it. She pulled away from him and stared.

"What's that?" she asked.

He pointed at the dogs. They were standing growling, their ruffs up. Then he spoke again, and as he spoke he crumpled to the ground. The dogs fell on him, so that she had to beat them off with her hands.

"Get away!" she shouted. "Who told you to kill him?"

And then, when they had slunk back, she heaved him somehow onto her back; and, trembling, half carrying, half pulling him, she dragged him to the ruined village and laid him in the street while she went to find her house, taking the dogs with her.

Her house was quite gone. She found the place easily enough. This was where it should be, opposite the water gate into the dike. She had always watched that gate herself. Miraculously it was not injured now, nor was the dike broken. It would be easy enough to rebuild the house. Only, for the present, it was gone.

So she went back to the young man. He was lying as she had left him, propped against the dike, panting and very pale. He had opened his coat and he had a little bag from which he was taking out strips of cloth and a bottle of something. And again he spoke, and again she understood nothing. Then he made signs and she saw it was water he wanted, so she took up a broken pot from one of many blown about the street, and, going up the dike, she filled it with river water and brought it down again and washed his wound, and she tore off the strips he made from the rolls of bandaging. He knew how to put the cloth over the gaping wound and he made signs to her, and she followed these signs. All the time he was trying to tell her something, but she could understand nothing.

"You must be from the South, sir," she said. It was easy to see that he had education. He looked very clever. "I have heard your language is different from ours." She laughed a little to put him at his ease, but he only stared at her somberly with dull eyes. So she said brightly, "Now if I could find something for us to eat, it would be nice."

He did not answer. Indeed he lay back, panting still more heavily, and stared into space as though she had not spoken.

"You would be better with food," she went on. "And so would I," she added. She was beginning to feel unbearably hungry.

It occurred to her that in Wang the baker's shop there might be some bread. Even if it were dusty with fallen mortar, it would still be bread. She would go and see. But before she went she moved the soldier a little so that he lay in the edge of shadow cast by a willow tree that grew in the bank of the dike. Then she went to the baker's shop. The dogs were gone.

The baker's shop was, like everything else, in ruins. No one was there. At first she saw nothing but the mass of crumpled earthen walls. But then she remembered that the oven was just inside the door, and the door frame still stood erect, supporting one end of the roof. She stood in this frame, and running her hand in underneath the fallen roof inside, she felt the wooden cover of the iron caldron. Under this there might be steamed bread. She worked her arm delicately and carefully in. It took quite a long time, but, even so, clouds of lime and dust almost choked her. Nevertheless she was right. She squeezed her hand under the cover and felt the firm smooth skin of the big steamed bread rolls, and one by one she drew out four.

"It's hard to kill an old thing like me," she remarked cheerfully to no one, and she began to eat one of the rolls as she walked back. If she had a bit of garlic and a bowl of tea — but one couldn't have everything in these times.

It was at this moment that she heard voices. When she came in sight of the soldier, she saw surrounding him a crowd of other soldiers, who had apparently come from nowhere. They were staring down at the wounded soldier, whose eyes were now closed.

"Where did you get this Japanese, Old Mother?" they shouted at her.

"What Japanese?" she asked.

"This one!" they shouted.

"Is he a Japanese?" she cried in the greatest astonishment. "But he looks like us — his eyes are black, his skin —"

"Japanese!" one of them shouted at her.

"Well," she said quietly, "he dropped out of the sky."

"Give me that bread!" another shouted.

"Take it," she said, "all except this one for him."

"A Japanese monkey eat good bread?" the soldier shouted.

"I suppose he is hungry also," old Mrs. Wang replied. She began to dislike these men. But then, she had always disliked soldiers.

"I wish you would go away," she said. "What are you doing here? Our village has always been peaceful."

"It certainly looks very peaceful now," one of the men said, grinning, "as peaceful as a grave. Do you know who did that, Old Mother? The Japanese!"

"I suppose so," she agreed. Then she asked. "Why? That's what I don't understand."

"Why? Because they want our land, that's why!"

"Our land!" she repeated. "Why, they can't have our land!"

"Never!" they shouted.

But all this time while they were talking and chewing the bread they had divided among themselves, they were watching the eastern horizon.

"Why do you keep looking east?" old Mrs. Wang now asked.

"The Japanese are coming from there," the man replied who had taken the bread.

"Are you running away from them?" she asked, surprised.

"There are only a handful of us," he said apologetically. "We were left to guard a village — Pao An, in the county of —"

"I know that village," old Mrs. Wang interrupted. "You needn't tell me. I was a girl there. How is the old Pao who keeps the teashop in the main street? He's my brother."

"Everybody is dead there," the man replied. "The Japanese have taken it—a great army of men came with their foreign guns and tanks, so what could we do?"

"Of course, only run," she agreed. Nevertheless she felt dazed and sick. So he was dead, that one brother she had left! She was now the last of her father's family.

But the soldiers were straggling away again leaving her alone.

"They'll be coming, those little black dwarfs," they were saying. "We'd best go on."

Nevertheless, one lingered a moment, the one who had taken the bread, to stare down at the young wounded man, who lay with his eyes shut, not having moved at all.

"Is he dead?" he inquired. Then, before Mrs. Wang could answer, he pulled a short knife out of his belt. "Dead or not, I'll give him a punch or two with this —"

But old Mrs. Wang pushed his arm away.

"No, you won't," she said with authority. "If he is dead, then there is no use in sending him into purgatory all in pieces. I am a good Buddhist myself."

The man laughed. "Oh well, he is dead," he answered, and then, seeing his comrades already at a distance, he ran after them.

A Japanese, was he? Old Mrs. Wang, left alone with this inert figure, looked at him tentatively. He was very young, she could see, now that his eyes were closed. His hand, limp in unconsciousness, looked like a boy's hand, unformed and still growing. She felt his wrist but could discern no pulse. She leaned over him and held to his lips the half of her roll which she had not eaten.

"Eat," she said very loudly and distinctly. "Bread!"

But there was no answer. Evidently he was dead. He must have died while she was getting the bread out of the oven.

There was nothing to do then but to finish the bread herself. And when that was done, she wondered if she ought not to follow after Little Pig and his wife and all the villagers. The sun was mounting and it was growing hot. If she were going, she had better go. But first she would climb the dike and see what the direction was. They had gone straight west, and as far as eye could look westward was a great plain. She might even see a good-sized crowd miles away. Anyway, she could see the next village, and they might all be there.

So she climbed the dike slowly, getting very hot. There was a slight breeze on top of the dike and it felt good. She was shocked to see the river very near the top of the dike. Why, it had risen in the last hour!

"You old demon!" she said severely. Let the river god hear it if he liked. He was evil, that he was—so to threaten flood when there had been all this other trouble.

She stooped and bathed her cheeks and her wrists. The water was quite cold, as though with fresh rains somewhere. Then she stood up and gazed around her. To the west there was nothing except in the far distance the soldiers still half-running, and beyond them the blur of the next village, which stood on a long rise of ground. She had better set out for that village. Doubtless Little Pig and his wife were there waiting for her.

Just as she was about to climb down and start out, she saw something on the eastern horizon. It was at first only an immense cloud of dust. But, as she stared at it, very quickly it became a lot of black dots and shining spots. Then she saw what it was. It was a lot of men—an army.

Instantly she knew what army.

"That's the Japanese," she thought. Yes, above them were the buzzing silver planes. They circled about, seeming to search for someone.

"I don't know who you're looking for," she muttered, "unless it's me and Little Pig and his wife. We're the only ones left. You've already killed my brother Pao."

She had almost forgotten that Pao was dead. Now she remembered it acutely. He had such a nice shop—always clean, and the tea good and the best meat dumplings to be had and the price always the same. Pao was a good man. Besides, what about his wife and his seven children? Doubtless they were all killed, too. Now these Japanese were looking for her. It occurred to her that on the dike she could easily be seen. So she clambered hastily down.

It was when she was about halfway down that she thought of the water gate. This old river — it had been a curse to them since time began. Why should it not make up a little now for all the wickedness it had done? It was plotting wickedness again, trying to steal over its banks. Well, why not? She wavered a moment. It was a pity, of course, that the young dead Japanese would be swept into the flood. He was a nice-looking boy, and she had saved him from being stabbed. It was not quite the same thing as saving his life, of course, but still it was a little the same. If he had been alive, he would have been saved. She went over to him and tugged at him until he lay well near the top of the bank. Then she went down again.

She knew perfectly how to open the water gate. Any child knew how to open the sluice for crops. But she knew also how to swing open the whole gate. The question was, could she open it quickly enough to get out of the way?

"I'm only one old woman," she muttered. She hesitated a second more. Well, it would be a pity not to see what sort of a baby Little Pig's wife would have, but one could not see everything. She had seen a great deal in this life. There was an end to what one could see, anyway.

She glanced again to the east. There were the Japanese coming across the plain. They were a long clear line of black, dotted with thousands of glittering points. If she opened this gate, the impetuous water would roar toward them, rushing into the plains, rolling into a wide lake, drowning them, maybe. Certainly they could not keep on marching nearer and nearer to her and to Little Pig and his wife who were waiting for her. Well, Little Pig and his wife — they would wonder about her—but they would never dream of this. It would make a good story — she would have enjoyed telling it.

She turned resolutely to the gate. Well, some people fought with airplanes and some with guns, but you could fight with a river, too, if it were a wicked one like this one. She wrenched out a huge wooden pin. It was slippery with silvery green moss. The rill of water burst into a strong jet. When she wrenched one more pin, the rest would give way themselves. She began pulling at it, and felt it slip a little from its hole.

"I might be able to get myself out of purgatory with this," she thought, "and maybe they'll let me have that old man of mine, too. What's a hand of his to all this? Then we'll —"

The pin slipped away suddenly, and the gate burst flat against her and knocked her breath away. She had only time to gasp, to the river:

"Come on, you old demon!"

Then she felt it seize her and lift her up to the sky. It was beneath her and around her. It rolled her joyfully hither and thither, and then, holding her close and enfolded, it went rushing against the enemy.

The Old Man at the Bridge

Ernest Hemingway

"I was taking care of animals," he said dully.
"I was only taking care of animals."

An old man with steel rimmed spectacles and very dusty clothes sat by the side of the road. There was a pontoon bridge across the river and carts, trucks, and men, women and children were crossing it. The mule-drawn carts staggered up the steep bank from the bridge with soldiers helping push against the spokes of the wheels. The trucks ground up and away heading out of it all and the peasants plodded along in the ankle deep dust. But the old man sat there without moving. He was too tired to go any farther.

It was my business to cross the bridge, explore the bridgehead beyond and find out to what point the enemy had advanced. I did this and returned over the bridge. There were not so many carts now and very few people on foot, but the old man was still there.

"Where do you come from?" I asked him.

"From San Carlos," he said, and smiled.

That was his native town and so it gave him pleasure to mention it and he smiled.

"I was taking care of animals," he explained.

"Oh," I said, not quite understanding.

"Yes," he said, "I stayed, you see, taking care of animals. I was the last one to leave the town of San Carlos."

He did not look like a shepherd nor a herdsman and I looked at his dusty clothes and his gray dusty face and his steel rimmed spectacles and said, "What animals were they?"

"Various animals," he said, and shook his head. "I had to leave them."

I was watching the bridge and the African-looking country of the Ebro Delta and wondering how long now it would be before we would see the enemy, and listening all the while for the first noises that would signal that ever mysterious event called contact, and the old man still sat there.

"What animals were they?" I asked.

"There were three animals altogether," he explained. "There were two goats and a cat and then there were four pairs of pigeons."

"And you had to leave them?" I asked.

"Yes. Because of the artillery. The captain told me to go because of the artillery."

"And you have no family?" I asked, watching the far end of the bridge where a few last carts were hurrying down the slope of the bank.

"No," he said "only the animals I stated. The cat, of course, will be all right. A cat can look out for itself, but I cannot think what will become of the others."

"What politics have you?" I asked.

"I am without politics," he said. "I am seventy-six years old. I have come twelve kilometres now and I think now I can go no further."

"This is not a good place to stop," I said. "If you can make it, there are trucks up the road where it forks for Tortosa."

"I will wait a while," he said, "and then I will go. Where do the trucks go?"

"Towards Barcelona," I told him.

"I know no one in that direction," he said, "but thank you very much. Thank you again very much."

He looked at me very blankly and tiredly, then said, having to share his worry with some one, "The cat will be all right, I am sure. There is no need to be unquiet about the cat. But the others. Now what do you think about the others?"

"Why they'll probably come through it all right."

"You think so?"

"Why not?" I said, watching the far bank where now there were no carts.

"But what will they do under the artillery when I was told to leave because of the artillery?"

"Did you leave the dove cage unlocked?" I asked.

"Yes."

"Then they'll fly."

"Yes, certainly they'll fly. But the others. It's better not to think about the others," he said.

"If you are rested I would go," I urged. "Get up and try to walk now."

"Thank you," he said and got to his feet, swayed from side to side and then sat down backwards in the dust.

"I was taking care of animals," he said dully, but no longer to me. "I was only taking care of animals."

There was nothing to do about him. It was Easter Sunday and the Fascists were advancing toward the Ebro. It was a gray overcast day with a low ceiling so their planes were not up. That and the fact that cats know how to look after themselves was all the good luck that old man would ever have.

The Cheat's Remorse

Morley Callaghan

"Watch me, lady," he said, and he spun the coin beautifully and it rolled in a wide arc on the table.

Phil was sipping a cup of coffee in Stewart's one night, sitting at the table near the radiator so that the snow would melt off his shoes and dry, when he saw a prosperous-looking hairy, blue-jowled man at the next table pushing a corned-beef sandwich on rye bread away from him slowly as if the sight of it made him sick. By the way the man sighed as he concentrated on the untouched sandwich anyone could see he was pretty drunk. He was clutching his food check firmly in his left hand as he used the other to tug and fumble at a roll of bills in his pocket. He was trying to get hold of himself, he was trying to get ready to walk up to the cashier in a straight line without stumbling, pay his check with dignity, and get into a taxi and home before he fell asleep.

The roll of bills that hung in the man's hand underneath the table as he leaned his weight forward staring at the cashier started Phil thinking how much he needed a dollar. He had been across the country and back on a bus, he was broke, his shirts were in a hand laundry on Twenty-sixth Street, and a man he had phoned yesterday, a man he had gone to school with, and who worked in a publisher's office now, had told him to come around and see him and he might be able to get him a few weeks' work in the shipping-room. But they wouldn't let him have the shirts at the laundry unless he paid for them. And he couldn't bear to see a man he had grown up with who was making a lot of money unless he had at least a clean shirt on.

As he leaned forward eagerly watching the man's thick fingers thumbing the roll of bills stiffly, trying to detach a bill while he concentrated on the goal which was the cashier's desk, the thing that Phil had hardly been daring to hope for happened: a bill was thumbed loose from the roll, the fat fingers clutched at it, missed it, and it fluttered in a little curve under the table and fell in the black smudge on the floor from the man's wet rubbers.

With a dreamy grin Phil kept looking beyond the man's head, beyond all the tables as if he were sniffing the rich odours from the food counter. But his heart gave a couple of jerks. And he had such a marvellously bright picture of himself going into the laundry in the morning and getting the shirts and putting on the light-blue one with a fine white stripe that he had paid seven dollars for a year ago.

But the drunk, having noticed him, was shaking his head at him. He was staring at Phil's battered felt hat and his old belted coat and his mussy shirt. He didn't like what he saw. It didn't help to make him feel secure and in full possession of himself. The dreamy look on Phil's face disgusted him.

"Hey, dreamy," he said, "what's eating you?"

"Me?"

"Yeah, you, dreamy."

"I wasn't looking at you. I'm making up my mind what I want."

"Excuse me, dreamy. Maybe you're right. I've been making mistakes all evening and I don't want to make any more," he said.

While he smiled very humbly at Phil a girl in a beige-coloured coat spotted with raindrops and snow, a girl with untidy fair hair that needed curling at the ends, and with good legs and a pale face, came over and sat down at his table. An unpunched food check was in her hand. She put her elbows on the table and looked around as if she were waiting for someone. The dollar bill on the floor was about two feet away from her foot.

The drunk rose from the table with considerable dignity and began to glide across the floor toward the cashier, his check held out with dreadful earnestness, his roll of bills tight in the other hand now. And when he had gone about twenty feet Phil glanced at the girl, their eyes met in a wary appraisal of each other, they looked steadily at each other, neither one moving, her eyes were blue and unwavering, and then, in spite of herself her glance shifted to the floor before she had time to move.

Phil got scared and lurched at the bill, one knee on the floor as he grabbed it, but she knew just where the bill was and her foot swung out and her toe held it down with all her weight, absolutely unyielding as he tugged at it, and he knew there was no chance of his getting even a piece of it unless he tore it. While he kept holding the edge of the bill he stared helplessly at her worn shoe that was wet, and then he looked at her ankle and at the run in her stocking that went half-way up the calf of her leg. He knew she was bending down. Her face was close to his.

"I guess it's a saw-off," he said, looking up.

"Looks like it," she said, her toe still on the bill, her face tense with eagerness.

"Maybe you want to run after him with it?"

"That wasn't in my mind," she said. She smiled a little in a bright, hard, unyielding way.

If she had taken her toe off the bill while they talked he mightn't have done the thing he did, but she made him feel she was only waiting for him to straighten up and be friendly to draw the bill closer to her; and the expectation of having the dollar and getting the shirt had given him quite a lift too, so he said, shrugging good-humouredly, "What do you think we should do?"

"What do you think yourself?"

"Tell you what I'll do," he said. "Figuring maybe we both saw it at the same time and that we both need it, how about if I toss you for it?"

She hesitated and said, "Seems fair enough. Go ahead."

They both smiled as he took a nickel from his vest pocket, and when she smiled like that he saw that she was quite young, there was a little bruise under her eye as though someone had hit her, but her face seemed to open out to him in spite of the pallor, the bruise and her untidy hair, and it was full of a sudden wild breathless eagerness. "Heads I win, tails you win," he said, getting ready to toss the coin.

"Let it land on the table and don't touch it and let it roll," she said, nodding her head and leaning forward.

"Watch me, lady," he said, and he spun the coin beautifully and it rolled in a wide arc on the table around the little stand that held the sugar, mustard, vinegar, and horse-radish sauce. When it stopped spinning they leaned forward so quickly their heads almost bumped.

"Heads, eh? Heads," she said, but she kept on looking down at it as if she couldn't see it. She was contemplating something, something in her head that was dreadful, a question maybe that found an answer in the coin on the table. Her face was close to his, and there were tears in her eyes, but she turned away and said faintly, "Okay, pal. It's all yours." She raised her foot and smiled a little while he bent down and picked up the bill.

"Thanks," he said. "Maybe you're lucky in love."

"Very likely. More power to you," she said, and she walked away and over to the cashier, where she handed in her unpunched food check.

He watched her raising the collar of her beige coat that was spotted from the rain and snow. A little bit of hair was caught and held outside the collar. While she was speaking to the cashier he was looking at the coin flat in the palm of his hand, looking at it and feeling dreadfully ashamed. He turned it over slowly and it was heads on both sides, the lucky phony coin he had found two years ago. And then he could hardly see the coin in his hand: he could see nothing but the expression on her face as she watched it spinning on the table, he heard her sigh, as if all the hope she had ever had in her life was put on the coin; he remembered how she had stiffened and then smiled: he felt that somehow her whole fate had depended on her having the bill. She had been close to it, just close enough to be tantalized, and then he had cheated her.

She was going out, and he rushed after her, and he saw her standing twenty feet away in the door of a cigar store. It was snowing again. She had walked through the snow; her bare shoes were carrying the snow as she stood there in the wet muddy entrance looking up and down the street. Before he could get near her she put hands deep in her pockets and started to walk away rapidly with her head down.

"Just a minute, lady. Hey, what's the hurry?" he called.

Unsmiling and wondering she turned and waited. "What's the matter with you?" she said.

"Do me a good turn, will you?"

"Why not if it don't hurt?"

"That depends on what it is," she said.

"Take the buck, will you, that's all," he said.

She tried to figure him out for a moment, then she said: "What is this, mister? You won it fair and square enough. Okay. Let it go at that." Her face looked much harder, suddenly much older than it had in the restaurant.

"No, I didn't win it on the level," he said. "Here, miss, take it, please," and he reached out and held her arm, but she pulled away from him, frowning. He grew flustered. "That was a phony coin I tossed, don't you see? I'll show it to you if you want to. You didn't have a chance."

"Then why the big heart now?" she said.

"I don't know. I was watching you go out and I got a hunch it was worse for you than it was for me. You had a bigger stake in it—" He went on pleading with her earnestly.

Mystified, she said, "Look here, if you cheated me you cheated me and I might have known it would be phony anyway, but—"

"I thought I needed the buck badly, but I felt lousy watching you go out. I needed to get my laundry tomorrow. I needed a clean shirt. That's what I was thinking watching the guy fingering the roll. And it was tough to see you come in on it. I didn't stop to think. I just went after it."

She was listening earnestly as if his remorse truly puzzled her, and then she put out her hand and gave him a pat on the arm that made him feel they knew each other well and had been together all evening, and that she was very old and he was just a green kid.

"Listen, you figure a clean shirt'll help you?" she said.

"I figured it would give me a head start, that's all."

"Maybe it will. Go ahead. Get the shirts."

"No, please, you take it."

"A clean shirt won't help me, nor the price of one," she said harshly. "So long," she said, with that bright, unyielding smile.

She walked away resolutely this time, as if she had made some final destructive decision, a decision she had dreaded and that she mightn't have made if he hadn't cheated her and she had got the dollar.

Worried, he went to run after her, but he stopped, startled and shaken, perceiving the truth as she had seen it, that a dollar in the long run was no good to her, that it would need a vast upheaval that shook the earth to really change the structure of her life. Yet she had been willing to stop and help him.

But the clean shirt became an absurd and trivial thing and the dollar felt unclean in his hand. He looked down the street at the tavern light. He had to get rid of the dollar or feel that he'd always see her walking away resolutely with her hands deep in her pockets.

Risk

Joanna Russ

**Medical advances had made it impossible
to die of anything . . .**

He didn't like this future world, oh no he didn't, our old friend John Hemingway London Rockne Knivel Dickey Wayne. It wasn't risky enough. He had been a racing-car driver way back then (before he was frozen) and he couldn't stand cars that protected you in head-on collisions and roads that wouldn't let you collide with anything in the first place. Nor did he like the medical advances which had made it impossible to die of anything (except extreme old age) or the sports they practised for health and fun (but never for danger). Nor was it possible to be better at something than anybody else. That is, you could be, but who cared? He wanted to go deep-sea diving, glider crashing, mountain-climbing, alligator-wrestling, lion-shooting, novel-writing, and even worse things. So he went before a parliament of these sensitive-but-bland men and women who had resurrected him from the cryogenics chambers of an earlier day and said loudly, legs planted far apart:

"LIFE IS NOT LIFE WITHOUT RISK!"

Then he said, even louder:

"MANKIND—IDENTITY—EVEN LIFE ITSELF—DEMANDS THE CONSTANT TEST OF DANGER!"

They said, "Oh dear." Their eyes got very round. They murmured worriedly amongst themselves. He thought he might have to throw a temper tantrum (the kind he used to put on so well in front of the news cameras) but that proved unnecessary. They debated politely. They put their hands over their faces. They said most of the unfrozen people seemed to like this new world. They said there really was no accounting for tastes, was there, after all.

But finally they said, "Very well; you shall have your Risk."

And they inoculated him with Bubonic Plague.

The Most Dangerous Game

Richard Connell

"You'll find this game worth playing," the
general said enthusiastically. "Your brain
against mine. Your strength and stamina
against mine. Outdoor chess. And the stake
is not without value, eh?"

"**O**ff there to the right — somewhere — is a large island," said
Whitney. "It's rather a mystery —"

"What island is it?" Rainsford asked.

"The old charts call it 'Ship-Trap Island'," Whitney replied. "A
suggestive name, isn't it? Sailors have a curious dread of the place.
I don't know why. Some superstition —"

"Can't see it," remarked Rainsford, trying to peer through the dank
tropical night that was palpable as it pressed its thick, warm blackness
in upon the yacht.

"You've good eyes," said Whitney, with a laugh, "and I've seen
you pick off a moose moving in the brown fall bush at four hundred
yards, but even you can't see four miles or so through a moonless
Caribbean night."

"Not four yards," admitted Rainsford. "Ugh! It's like moist black
velvet."

"It will be light enough where we're going," promised Whitney.
"We should make it in a few days. I hope the jaguar guns have come.
We'll have good hunting up the Amazon. Great sport, hunting."

"The best sport in the world," agreed Rainsford.

"For the hunter," amended Whitney. "Not for the jaguar."

"Don't talk rot, Whitney," said Rainsford. "You're a big game
hunter, not a philosopher. Who cares how a jaguar feels?"

"Perhaps the jaguar does," observed Whitney.

"Bah! They've no understanding."

"Even so, I rather think they understand one thing—fear. The fear of pain and the fear of death."

"Nonsense," laughed Rainsford. "This hot weather is making you soft, Whitney. Be a realist. The world is made up of two classes—the hunters and the hunted. Luckily, you and I are hunters. Do you think we've passed that island yet?"

"I can't tell in the dark. I hope so."

"Why?" asked Rainsford.

"The place has a reputation — a bad one."

"Cannibals?" suggested Rainsford.

"Hardly. Even cannibals wouldn't live in such a God-forsaken place. But it's got into sailor lore, somehow. Didn't you notice that the crew's nerves seemed a bit jumpy today?"

"They were a bit strange, now that you mention it. Even Captain Nielsen —"

"Yes, even that tough-minded old Swede, who'd go up to the devil himself and ask him for a light. Those fishy blue eyes held a look I never saw there before. All I could get out of him was: 'This place has an evil name among seafaring men, sir.' Then he said to me, very gravely: 'Don't you feel anything?'—as if the air about us was actually poisonous. Now, you mustn't laugh when I tell you this — I did feel something like a sudden chill.

"There was no breeze. The sea was as flat as a plate-glass window. We were drawing near the island then. What I felt was a mental chill; a sort of sudden dread."

"Pure imagination," said Rainsford. "One superstitious sailor can taint the whole ship's company with his fear."

"Maybe. But sometimes I think sailors have an extra sense that tells them when they are in danger. Sometimes I think evil is a tangible thing—with wave lengths, just as sound and light have. An evil place can, so to speak, broadcast vibrations of evil. Anyhow, I'm glad we're getting out of this zone. Well, I think I'll turn in now, Rainsford."

"I'm not sleepy," said Rainsford. "I'm going to smoke another pipe up on the afterdeck."

"Good night, then, Rainsford. See you at breakfast."

"Right. Good night, Whitney."

There was no sound in the night as Rainsford sat there, but the muffled throb of the engine that drove the yacht swiftly through the darkness, and the swish and ripple of the wash of the propeller.

Rainsford, reclining in a steamer chair, indolently puffed on his favorite briar. The sensuous drowsiness of the night was on him.

"It's so dark," he thought, "that I could sleep without closing my eyes; the night would be my eyelids —"

An abrupt sound startled him. Off to the right he heard it, and his ears, expert in such matters, could not be mistaken. Again he heard the sound, and again. Somewhere, off in the blackness, someone had fired a gun three times.

Rainsford sprang up and moved quickly to the rail, mystified. He strained his eyes in the direction from which the reports had come, but it was like trying to see through a blanket. He leaped upon the rail and balanced himself there, to get greater elevation; his pipe, striking a rope, was knocked from his mouth. He lunged for it; a short, hoarse cry came from his lips as he realized he had reached too far and had lost his balance. The cry was pinched off short as the blood-warm waters of the Caribbean Sea closed over his head.

He struggled up to the surface and tried to cry out, but the wash from the speeding yacht slapped him in the face and the salt water in his open mouth made him gag and strangle. Desperately he struck out with strong strokes after the receding lights of the yacht, but he stopped before he had swum fifty feet. A certain cool-headedness had come to him; it was not the first time he had been in a tight place. There was a chance that his cries could be heard by someone aboard the yacht, but that chance was slender, and grew more slender as the yacht raced on. He wrestled himself out of his clothes, and shouted with all his power. The lights of the yacht became faint and ever-vanishing fireflies; then they were blotted out entirely by the night.

Rainsford remembered the shots. They had come from the right, and doggedly he swam in that direction, swimming with slow, deliberate strokes, conserving his strength. For a seemingly endless time he fought the sea. He began to count his strokes; he could do possibly a hundred more and then —

Rainsford heard a sound. It came out of the darkness, a high screaming sound, the sound of an animal in an extremity of anguish and terror.

He did not recognize the animal that made the sound—he did not try to; with fresh vitality he swam toward the sound. He heard it again; then it was cut short by another noise, crisp, staccato.

"Pistol shot," muttered Rainsford, swimming on.

Ten minutes of determined effort brought another sound to his ears —the most welcome he had ever heard—the muttering and growling of the sea breaking on a rocky shore. He was almost on the rocks before he saw them; on a night less calm he would have been shattered against them. With his remaining strength he dragged himself from the swirling waters. Jagged crags appeared to jut into the opaqueness; he forced himself upward, hand over hand. Gasping, his hands raw, he reached a flat place at the top. Dense jungle came down to the very edge of the cliffs. What perils that tangle of trees and underbrush might hold for him did not concern Rainsford just then. All he knew was that he was safe from his enemy, the sea, and that utter weariness was on him. He flung himself down at the jungle edge and tumbled headlong into the deepest sleep of his life.

When he opened his eyes he knew from the position of the sun that it was late in the afternoon. Sleep had given him new vigor; a sharp hunger was picking at him. He looked about him, almost cheerfully.

"Where there are pistol shots, there are men. Where there are men, there is food," he thought. But what kind of men, he wondered, in so forbidding a place? An unbroken front of snarled and jagged jungle fringed the shore.

He saw no sign of a trail through the closely knit web of weeds and trees; it was easier to go along the shore, and Rainsford floundered along by the water. Not far from where he had landed, he stopped.

Some wounded thing, by the evidence a large animal, had thrashed about in the underbrush. The jungle weeds were crushed down and the moss was lacerated; one patch of weeds was stained crimson. A small, glittering object not far away caught Rainsford's eye and he picked it up. It was an empty cartridge.

"A twenty-two," he remarked. "That's odd. It must have been a fairly large animal too. The hunter had his nerve with him to tackle it with such a light gun. It's clear that the brute put up a good fight. I suppose the first three shots I heard were when the hunter flushed his quarry and wounded it. The last shot was when he trailed it here and finished it."

He examined the ground closely and found what he had hoped to find—the print of hunting-boots. They pointed along the cliff in the direction he had been going. Eagerly he hurried along, now slipping

on a rotten log or a loose stone, but making headway; night was beginning to settle down on the island.

Bleak darkness was blacking out the sea and jungle when Rainsford sighted the lights. He came upon them as he turned a crook in the coast line, and his first thought was that he had come upon a village, for there were many lights. But as he forged along he saw to his great astonishment that all the lights were in one enormous building — a lofty structure with pointed towers plunging upward into the gloom. His eyes made out the shadowy outlines of a palatial château; it was set on a high bluff, and on three sides of it cliffs dived down to where the sea licked greedy lips in the shadows.

"Mirage," thought Rainsford. But it was no mirage, he found, when he opened the tall spiked iron gate. The stone steps were real enough. The massive door with a leering gargoyle for a knocker was real enough. Yet about it all hung an air of unreality.

He lifted the knocker, and it creaked up stiffly, as if it had never before been used. He let it fall, and it startled him with its booming loudness. He thought he heard steps within; the door remained closed. Again Rainsford lifted the heavy knocker, and let it fall. The door opened then, opened as suddenly as if it were on a spring, and Rainsford stood blinking in the river of glaring gold light that poured out. The first thing Rainsford's eyes discerned was the largest man he had ever seen — a gigantic creature, solidly made and black-bearded to the waist. In his hand the man held a long-barreled revolver, and he was pointing it straight at Rainsford's heart.

Out of the snarl of beard two small eyes regarded Rainsford.

"Don't be alarmed," said Rainsford, with a smile which he hoped was disarming. "I'm no robber. I fell off a yacht. My name is Sanger Rainsford of New York City."

The menacing look in the eyes did not change. The revolver pointed as rigidly as if the giant were a statue. He gave no sign that he understood Rainsford's words, or that he had even heard them. He was dressed in uniform, a black uniform trimmed with gray astrakhan.

"I'm Sanger Rainsford of New York," Rainsford began again. "I fell off a yacht. I am hungry."

The man's only answer was to raise with his thumb the hammer of his revolver. Then Rainsford saw the man's free hand go to his forehead in a military salute, and he saw him click his heels together and stand at attention. Another man was coming down the broad marble steps, an erect, slender man in evening clothes. He advanced and held out his hand.

In a cultivated voice marked by a slight accent that gave it added precision and deliberateness, he said: "It is a very great pleasure and honor to welcome Mr. Sanger Rainsford, the celebrated hunter, to my home." Automatically Rainsford shook the man's hand.

"I've read your book about hunting snow leopards in Tibet, you see," explained the man. "I am General Zaroff."

Rainsford's first impression was that the man was singularly handsome; his second was that there was an original, almost bizarre quality about the general's face. He was a tall man past middle age, for his hair was a vivid white; but his thick eyebrows and pointed military mustache were as black as the night from which Rainsford had come. His eyes, too, were black and very bright. He had high cheekbones, a sharp-cut nose, a spare, dark face, the face of a man used to giving orders, the face of an aristocrat. Turning to the giant in uniform, the general made a sign. The giant put away his pistol, saluted, withdrew.

"Ivan is an incredibly strong fellow," remarked the general, "but he has the misfortune to be deaf and dumb. A simple fellow, but, I'm afraid, like all his race, a bit of a savage."

"Is he Russian?"

"He is a Cossack," said the general, and his smile showed red lips and pointed teeth. "So am I.

"Come," he said, "we shouldn't be chatting here. We can talk later. Now you want clothes, food, rest. You shall have them. This is a most restful spot."

Ivan had reappeared, and the general spoke to him with lips that moved but gave forth no sound.

"Follow Ivan, if you please, Mr. Rainsford," said the general. "I was about to have my dinner when you came. I'll wait for you. You'll find that my clothes will fit you, I think."

It was to a huge, beam-ceilinged bedroom with a canopied bed big enough for six men that Rainsford followed the silent giant. Ivan laid out an evening suit, and Rainsford, as he put it on, noticed that it came from a London tailor who ordinarily cut and sewed for none below the rank of duke.

The dining room to which Ivan conducted him was in many ways remarkable. There was a medieval magnificence about it; it suggested a baronial hall of feudal times with its oaken panels, its high ceiling, its vast refectory table where twoscore men could sit down to eat. About the hall were the mounted heads of many animals — lions, tigers, elephants, moose, bears; larger or more perfect specimens Rainsford had never seen. At the great table the general was sitting alone.

"You'll have a cocktail, Mr. Rainsford," he suggested. The cocktail was surpassingly good; and, Rainsford noted, the table appointments were of the finest — the linen, the crystal, the silver, the china.

They were eating *borsch*, the rich, red soup with whipped cream so dear to Russian palates. Half apologetically General Zaroff said: "We do our best to preserve the amenities of civilization here. Please forgive any lapses. We are well off the beaten track, you know. Do you think the champagne has suffered from its long ocean trip?"

"Not in the least," declared Rainsford. He was finding the general a most thoughtful and affable host, a true cosmopolite. But there was one trait of the general's that made Rainsford uncomfortable. Whenever he looked up he found the general studying him, appraising him narrowly.

"Perhaps," said General Zaroff, "you were surprised that I recognized your name. You see, I read all books on hunting published in English, French, and Russian. I have but one passion in my life, Mr. Rainsford, and it is the hunt."

"You have some wonderful heads here," said Rainsford as he ate a particularly well-cooked filet mignon. "That Cape buffalo is the largest I ever saw."

"Oh, that fellow. Yes, he was a monster."

"Did he charge you?"

"Hurled me against a tree," said the general. "Fractured my skull. But I got the brute."

"I've always thought," said Rainsford, "that the Cape buffalo is the most dangerous of all big game."

For a moment the general did not reply; he was smiling his curious red-lipped smile. Then he said slowly: "No. You are wrong, sir. The Cape buffalo is not the most dangerous big game." He sipped his wine. "Here in my preserve on this island," he said in the same slow tone, "I hunt more dangerous game."

Rainsford expressed his surprise. "Is there big game on this island?"

The general nodded. "The biggest."

"Really?"

"Oh, it isn't here naturally, of course. I have to stock the island."

"What have you imported, General?" Rainsford asked. "Tigers?"

The general smiled. "No," he said. "Hunting tigers ceased to interest me some years ago. I exhausted their possibilities, you see. No thrill left in tigers, no real danger. I live for danger, Mr. Rainsford."

The general took from his pocket a gold cigarette case and offered his guest a long black cigarette with a silver tip; it was perfumed and gave off a smell like incense.

"We will have some capital hunting, you and I," said the general. "I shall be most glad to have your society."

"But what game —" began Rainsford.

"I'll tell you," said the general. "You will be amused, I know. I think I may say, in all modesty, that I have done a rare thing. I have invented a new sensation. May I pour you another glass of port, Mr. Rainsford?"

"Thank you, General."

The general filled both glasses, and said: "God makes some men poets. Some He makes kings, some beggars. Me He made a hunter. My hand was made for the trigger, my father said. He was a very rich man with a quarter of a million acres in the Crimea, and he was an ardent sportsman. When I was only five years old he gave me a little gun, specially made in Moscow for me, to shoot sparrows with. When

I shot some of his prize turkeys with it, he did not punish me; he complimented me on my marksmanship. I killed my first bear in the Caucasus when I was ten. My whole life had been one prolonged hunt. I went into the army—it was expected of noblemen's sons—and for a time commanded a division of Cossack cavalry, but my real interest was always the hunt. I have hunted every kind of game in every land. It would be impossible for me to tell you how many animals I have killed."

The general puffed at his cigarette.

"After the debacle in Russia I left the country, for it was imprudent for an officer of the Czar to stay there. Many noble Russians lost everything. I, luckily, had invested heavily in American securities, so I shall never have to open a tearoom in Monte Carlo or drive a taxi in Paris. Naturally, I continued to hunt — grizzlies in your Rockies, crocodiles in the Ganges, rhinoceroses in East Africa. It was in Africa that the Cape buffalo hit me and laid me up for six months. As soon as I recovered I started for the Amazon to hunt jaguars, for I had heard they were unusually cunning. They weren't." The Cossack sighed. "They were no match at all for a hunter with his wits about him, and a high-powered rifle. I was bitterly disappointed. I was lying in my tent with a splitting headache one night when a terrible thought pushed its way into my mind. Hunting was beginning to bore me! And hunting, remember, had been my life. I have heard that in America businessmen often go to pieces when they give up the business that has been their life."

"Yes, that's so," said Rainsford.

The general smiled. "I had no wish to go to pieces," he said. "I must do something. Now, mine is an analytical mind, Mr. Rainsford. Doubtless that is why I enjoy the problems of the chase."

"No doubt, General Zaroff."

"So," continued the general, "I asked myself why the hunt no longer fascinated me. You are much younger than I am, Mr. Rainsford, and have not hunted as much, but you perhaps can guess the answer."

"What was it?"

"Simply this: hunting had ceased to be what you call 'a sporting proposition'. It had become too easy. I always got my quarry. Always. There is no greater bore than perfection."

The general lit a fresh cigarette.

"No animal had a chance with me any more. That is no boast;

it is a mathematical certainty. The animal had nothing but his legs and his instinct. Instinct is no match for reason. When I thought of this it was a tragic moment for me, I can tell you."

Rainsford leaned across the table, absorbed in what his host was saying.

"It came to me as an inspiration what I must do," the general went on.

"And that was?"

The general smiled the quiet smile of one who has faced an obstacle and surmounted it with success. "I had to invent a new animal to hunt," he said.

"A new animal? You're joking."

"Not at all," said the general. "I never joke about hunting. I needed a new animal. I found one. So I bought this island, built this house, and here I do my hunting. The island is perfect for my purposes—there are jungles with a maze of trails in them, hills, swamps —"

"But the animal, General Zaroff?"

"Oh," said the general, "it supplies me with the most exciting hunting in the world. No other hunting compares with it for an instant. Every day I hunt, and I never grow bored now, for I have a quarry with which I can match my wits."

Rainsford's bewilderment showed in his face.

"I wanted the ideal animal to hunt," explained the general. "So I said: 'What are the attributes of an ideal quarry?' And the answer was, of course: 'It was must have courage, cunning, and, above all, it must be able to reason.' "

"But no animal can reason," objected Rainsford.

"My dear fellow," said the general, "there is one that can."

"But you can't mean —," gasped Rainsford.

"And why not?"

"I can't believe you are serious, General Zaroff. This is a grisly joke."

"Why should I not be serious? I am speaking of hunting."

"Hunting? Good God, General Zaroff, what you speak of is murder."

The general laughed with entire good nature. He regarded Rainsford quizzically. "I refuse to believe that so modern and civilized a young man as you harbors romantic ideas about the value of human life. Surely your experiences in the war —"

"Did not make me condone cold-blooded murder," finished

Rainsford stiffly.

Laughter shook the general. "How extraordinarily droll you are!" he said. "One does not expect nowadays to find a young man of the educated class, even in America, with such a naive and, if I may say so, mid-Victorian point of view. It's like finding a snuffbox in a limousine. Ah, well, doubtless you had Puritan ancestors. So many Americans appear to have had. I'll wager you'll forget your notions when you go hunting with me. You've a genuine thrill in store for you, Mr. Rainsford."

"Thank you, I'm a hunter, not a murderer."

"Dear me," said the general, quite unruffled, "again that unpleasant word. But I think I can show you that your scruples are quite unfounded."

"Yes?"

"Life is for the strong, to be lived by the strong, and, if needs be, taken by the strong. The weak of the world were put here to give the strong pleasure. I am strong. Why should I not use my gift? If I wish to hunt, why should I not? I hunt the scum of the earth. A thoroughbred horse or hound is worth more than a score of them."

"But they are men," said Rainsford hotly.

"Precisely," said the general. "That is why I use them. It gives me pleasure. They can reason, after a fashion. So they are dangerous."

"But where do you get them?"

The general's eyelid fluttered down in a wink. "This island is called 'Ship-Trap'," he answered. "Sometimes an angry god of the high seas sends them to me. Sometimes, when Providence is not so kind, I help Providence a bit. Come to the window with me."

Rainsford went to the window and looked out toward the sea.

"Watch! Out there!" exclaimed the general, pointing into the night. Rainsford's eyes saw only blackness, and then, as the general pressed a button, far out to sea Rainsford saw the flash of lights.

The general chuckled. "They indicate a channel," he said, "where there's none: giant rocks with razor edges crouch like a sea monster with wide open jaws. They can crush a ship as easily as I crush this nut." He dropped a walnut on the hardwood floor and brought his heel grinding down on it. "Oh, yes," he said, casually, as if in answer to a question, "I have electricity. We try to be civilized here."

"Civilized? And you shoot down men."

A trace of anger was in the general's black eyes, but it was there for but a second, and he said, in his most pleasant manner: "Dear me, what a righteous young man you are! I assure you I do not do the thing you suggest. That would be barbarous. I treat these visitors with every consideration. They get plenty of good food and exercise. They get into splendid physical condition. You shall see for yourself tomorrow."

"What do you mean?"

"We'll visit my training school," smiled the general. "It's in the cellar. I have about a dozen pupils down there now. They're from the Spanish bark, *San Lucar,* that had the bad luck to go on the rocks out there. A very inferior lot, I regret to say. Poor specimens and more accustomed to the deck than to the jungle."

He raised his hand, and Ivan, who served as waiter, brought thick Turkish coffee. Rainsford, with an effort, held his tongue in check.

"It's a game, you see," pursued the general blandly. "I suggest to one of them that we go hunting. I give him a supply of food and an excellent hunting knife. I give him three hours' start. I am to follow, armed only with a pistol of the smallest caliber and range. If my quarry eludes me for three whole days, he wins the game. If I find him," the general smiled, "he loses."

"Suppose he refuses to be hunted?"

"Oh," said the general, "I give him his option, of course. He need not play that game if he doesn't wish to. If he does not wish to hunt I turn him over to Ivan. Ivan once had the honor of serving as official knouter to the Great White Czar, and he has his own ideas of sport. Invariably, Mr. Rainsford, invariably they choose the hunt."

"And if they win?"

The smile on the general's face widened. "To date I have not lost," he said.

Then he added, hastily: "I don't wish you to think me a braggart, Mr. Rainsford. Many of them afford only the most elementary sort of problem. Occasionally I strike a tartar. One almost did win. I eventually had to use the dogs."

"The dogs?"

"This way, please. I'll show you."

The general steered Rainsford to a window. The lights from the window sent a flickering illumination that made grotesque patterns on the courtyard below, and Rainsford could see moving about there a dozen or so huge black shapes; as they turned toward him, their eyes glittered greenly.

"A rather good lot, I think," observed the general. "They are let out at seven every night. If anyone should try to get into my house — or out of it — something extremely regrettable would occur to him." He hummed a snatch of song from the Folies Bergère.

"And now," said the general, "I want to show you my new collection of heads. Will you come with me to the library?"

"I hope," said Rainsford, "that you will excuse me tonight, General Zaroff. I'm really not feeling at all well."

"Ah, indeed?" the general inquired solicitously. "Well, I suppose that's only natural, after your long swim. You need a good, restful night's sleep. Tomorrow you'll feel like a new man, I'll wager. Then we'll hunt, eh? I've one rather promising prospect —"

Rainsford was hurrying from the room.

"Sorry you can't go with me tonight," called the general. "I expect rather fair sport — a big, strong man. He looks resourceful. Well, good night, Mr. Rainsford. I hope you have a good night's rest."

The bed was good and the pajamas of the softest silk, and he was tired in every fiber of his being, but nevertheless Rainsford could not quiet his brain with the opiate of sleep. He lay, eyes wide open. Once he thought he heard stealthy steps in the corridor outside his room. He sought to throw open the door; it would not open. He went to the window and looked out. His room was high up in one of the towers. The lights of the château were out now, and it was dark and silent, but there was a fragment of sallow moon, and by its wan light he could see, dimly, the courtyard. There, weaving in and out in the pattern of shadow, were black, noiseless forms; the hounds heard him at the window and looked up, expectantly, with their green eyes. Rainsford went back to the bed and lay down. By many methods he tried to put himself to sleep. He had achieved a doze when, just as morning began to come, he heard, far off in the jungle, the faint report of a pistol.

General Zaroff did not appear until luncheon. He was dressed faultlessly in the tweeds of a country squire. He was solicitous about the state of Rainsford's health.

"As for me," sighed the general, "I do not feel so well. I am worried, Mr. Rainsford. Last night I detected traces of my old complaint."

To Rainsford's questioning glance the general said: "Ennui. Boredom."

Then, taking a second helping of crêpe suzette, the general explained: "The hunting was not good last night. The fellow lost his head. He made a straight trail that offered no problems at all. That's the trouble with these sailors; they have dull brains to begin with, and they do not know how to get about in the woods. They do excessively stupid and obvious things. It's most annoying. Will you have another glass of Chablis, Mr. Rainsford?"

"General," said Rainsford firmly, "I wish to leave this island at once."

The general raised his thickets of eyebrows; he seemed hurt. "But, my dear fellow," the general protested, "you've only just come. You've had no hunting —"

"I wish to go today," said Rainsford. He saw the dead black eyes of the general on him, studying him. General Zaroff's face suddenly brightened.

He filled Rainsford's glass with venerable Chablis from a dusty bottle.

"Tonight," said the general, "we will hunt — you and I."

Rainsford shook his head. "No, General," he said. "I will not hunt."

The general shrugged his shoulders and nibbled delicately at a hothouse grape. "As you wish, my friend," he said. "The choice rests entirely with you. But may I not venture to suggest that you will find my idea of sport more diverting than Ivan's?"

He nodded toward the corner where the giant stood, scowling, his thick arms crossed on his hogshead of chest.

"You don't mean —" cried Rainsford.

"My dear fellow," said the general, "have I not told you I always mean what I say about hunting? This is really an inspiration. I drink to a foeman worthy of my steel — at last."

The general raised his glass, but Rainsford sat staring at him.

"You'll find this game worth playing," the general said enthusiastically. "Your brain against mine. Your woodcraft against mine. Your strength and stamina against mine. Outdoor chess. And the stake is not without value, eh?"

"And if I win —" began Rainsford huskily.

"I'll cheerfully admit myself defeated if I do not find you by midnight of the third day," said General Zaroff. "My sloop will place you on the mainland near a town."

The general read what Rainsford was thinking.

"Oh, you can trust me," said the Cossack. "I will give you my word as a gentleman and a sportsman. Of course, you, in turn, must agree to say nothing of your visit here."

"I'll agree to nothing of the kind," said Rainsford.

"Oh," said the general, "in that case — but why discuss that now? Three days hence we can discuss it over a bottle of Veuve Cliquot, unless —"

The general sipped his wine.

Then a businesslike air animated him. "Ivan," he said to Rainsford, "will supply you with hunting clothes, food, a knife. I suggest you wear moccasins; they leave a poorer trail. I should suggest too that you avoid the big swamp in the southeast corner of the island. We call it Death Swamp. There's quicksand there. One foolish fellow tried it. The deplorable part of it was that Lazarus followed him. You can imagine my feelings, Mr. Rainsford. I loved Lazarus; he was the finest hound in my pack. Well, I must beg you to excuse me now. I always take a siesta after lunch. You'll hardly have time for a nap, I fear. You'll want to start, no doubt. I shall not follow till dusk. Hunting at night is so much more exciting than by day, don't you think? Au revoir, Mr. Rainsford, au revoir."

General Zaroff, with a deep, courtly bow, strolled from the room.

From another door came Ivan. Under one arm he carried khaki hunting clothes, a haversack of food, a leather sheath containing a long-bladed hunting knife; his right hand rested on a cocked revolver thrust in the crimson sash around his waist. . . .

Rainsford had fought his way through the bush for two hours.

"I must keep my nerve. I must keep my nerve," he said through tight teeth.

He had not been entirely clear-headed when the château gates snapped shut behind him. His whole idea at first was to put distance between himself and General Zaroff, and, to this end, he had plunged along, spurred on by the sharp rowels of something very like panic. Now he had got a grip on himself, had stopped, and was taking stock of himself and the situation.

He saw that straight flight was futile; inevitably it would bring him face to face with the sea. He was in a picture with a frame of water, and his operations, clearly, must take place within that frame.

"I'll give him a trail to follow," muttered Rainsford, and he struck

off from the rude path he had been following into the trackless
wilderness. He executed a series of intricate loops; he doubled on his
trail again and again, recalling all the lore of the fox hunt, and all the
dodges of the fox. Night found him leg-weary, with hands and face
lashed by the branches, on a thickly wooded ridge. He knew it would
be insane to blunder on through the dark, even if he had the strength.
His need for rest was imperative and he thought: "I have played the
fox, now I must play the cat of the fable." A big tree with a thick trunk
and outspread branches was near by, and, taking care to leave not the
slightest mark, he climbed up into the crotch, and stretching out on
one of the broad limbs, after a fashion, rested. Rest brought him new
confidence and almost a feeling of security. Even so zealous a hunter as
General Zaroff could not trace him there, he told himself; only the
devil himself could follow that complicated trail through the jungle
after dark. But, perhaps, the general was a devil. . . .

An apprehensive night crawled slowly by like a wounded snake, and
sleep did not visit Rainsford, although the silence of a dead world was
on the jungle. Toward morning when a dingy gray was varnishing the
sky, the cry of some startled bird focused Rainsford's attention in that
direction. Something was coming through the bush, coming slowly,
carefully, coming by the same winding way Rainsford had come. He
flattened himself down on the limb, and through a screen of leaves
almost as thick as tapestry, he watched. The thing that was approach-
ing was a man.

It was General Zaroff. He made his way along with his eyes fixed in
utmost concentration on the ground before him. He paused almost
beneath the tree, dropped to his knees, and studied the ground before
him. Rainsford's impulse was to hurl himself down like a panther,
but he saw that the general's right hand held something small and
metallic — an automatic pistol.

The hunter shook his head several times as if he were puzzled. Then
he straightened up and took from his case one of his black cigarettes;
its pungent incenselike smoke floated up to Rainsford's nostrils.

Rainsford held his breath. The general's eyes had left the ground
and were traveling inch by inch up the tree. Rainsford froze there,
every muscle tensed for a spring. But the sharp eyes of the hunter
stopped before they reached the limb where Rainsford lay; a smile
spread over his brown face. Very deliberately he blew a smoke ring
into the air; then he turned his back on the tree and walked carelessly

away, back along the trail he had come. The swirls of the underbrush against his hunting boots grew fainter and fainter.

The pent-up air burst hotly from Rainsford's lungs. His first thought made him feel sick and numb. The general could follow a trail through the woods at night, he could follow an extremely difficult trail. He must have uncanny powers; only by the merest chance had the Cossack failed to see his quarry.

Rainsford's second thought was even more terrible. It sent a shudder of cold through his whole being. Why had the general smiled? Why had he turned back?

Rainsford did not want to believe what his reason told him was true, but the truth was as evident as the sun that had by now pushed through the morning mists. The general was playing with him. The general was saving him for another day's sport! The Cossack was the cat; he was the mouse. Then it was that Rainsford knew the full meaning of terror.

"I will not lose my nerve. I will not."

He slid down from the tree, and struck off again into the woods. His face was set and he forced the machinery of his mind to function. Three hundred yards from his hiding place he stopped where a huge dead tree leaned precariously on a smaller living one. Throwing off his sack of food, Rainsford took his knife from its sheath and began to work with all his energy.

The job was finished at last, and he threw himself down behind a fallen log a hundred feet away. He did not have to wait long. The cat was coming again to play with the mouse.

Following the trail with the sureness of a bloodhound came General Zaroff. Nothing escaped those searching black eyes, no crushed blade of grass, no bent twig, no mark, no matter how faint, in the moss. So intent was the Cossack on his stalking that he was upon the thing Rainsford had made before he saw it. His foot touched the protruding bough that was the trigger. Even as he touched it, the general sensed his danger and leaped back with the agility of an ape. But he was not quite quick enough; the dead tree, delicately adjusted to rest on the cut living one, crashed down and struck the general a glancing blow on the shoulder as it fell. But for his alertness, he would have been smashed beneath it. He staggered, but he did not fall; nor did he drop his revolver. He stood there rubbing his injured shoulder, and Rainsford, with fear again gripping his heart, heard the general's mocking laugh ring through the jungle.

"Rainsford," called the general, "if you are within sound of my voice, as I suppose you are, let me congratulate you. Not many men know how to make a Malay man-catcher. Luckily, for me, I too have hunted in Malacca. You are proving interesting, Mr. Rainsford. I am going now to have my wound dressed; it's only a slight one. But I shall be back. I shall be back."

When the general, nursing his bruised shoulder, had gone, Rainsford took up his flight again. It was flight now, a desperate, hopeless flight, that carried him on for some hours. Dusk came, then darkness, and still he pressed on. The ground grew softer under his moccasins; the vegetation grew ranker, denser; insects bit him savagely. Then as he stepped forward, his foot sank into the ooze. He tried to wrench it back, but the muck sucked viciously at his foot as if it were a giant leech. With a violent effort, he tore his foot loose. He knew where he was now. Death Swamp and its quicksand.

His hands were tight closed as if his nerve were something tangible that someone in the darkness was trying to tear from his grip. The softness of the earth had given him an idea. He stepped back from the quicksand a dozen feet or so and, like some huge prehistoric beaver, he began to dig.

Rainsford had dug himself in in France when a second's delay meant death. That had been a placid pastime compared to his digging now. The pit grew deeper; when it was above his shoulders, he climbed out and from some hard saplings cut stakes and sharpened them to a fine point. These stakes he planted in the bottom of the pit with the points sticking up. With flying fingers he wove a rough carpet of weeds and branches and with it he covered the mouth of the pit. Then, wet with sweat and aching with tiredness, he crouched behind the stump of a lightning-charred tree.

He knew his pursuer was coming; he heard the padding sound of feet on the soft earth, and the night breeze brought him the perfume of the general's cigarette. It seemed to Rainsford that the general was coming with unusual swiftness; he was not feeling his way along, foot by foot. Rainsford, crouching there, could not see the general, nor could he see the pit. He lived a year in a minute. Then he felt an impulse to cry aloud with joy, for he heard the sharp crackle of the breaking branches as the cover of the pit gave way; he heard the sharp scream of pain as the pointed stakes found their mark. He leaped up from his place of concealment. Then he cowered back. Three feet from the pit a man was standing, with an electric torch in his hand.

"You've done well, Rainsford," the voice of the general called. "Your Burmese tiger pit has claimed one of my best dogs. Again you score. I think, Mr. Rainsford, I'll see what you can do against my whole pack. I'm going home for a rest now. Thank you for a most amusing evening."

At daybreak Rainsford, lying near the swamp, was awakened by a sound that made him know that he had new things to learn about fear. It was a distant sound, faint and wavering, but he knew it. It was the baying of a pack of hounds.

Rainsford knew he could do one of two things. He could stay where he was and wait. That was suicide. He could flee. That was postponing the inevitable. For a moment he stood there, thinking. An idea that held a wild chance came to him, and, tightening his belt, he headed away from the swamp. The baying of the hounds drew nearer, then still nearer, nearer, ever nearer. On a ridge Rainsford climbed a tree. Down a watercourse, not a quarter of a mile away, he could see the bush moving. Straining his eyes, he saw the lean figure whose wide

shoulders surged through the tall jungle weeds; it was the giant Ivan, and he seemed pulled forward by some unseen force. Rainsford knew that Ivan must be holding the pack in leash.

They would be on him any minute now. His mind worked frantically. He thought of a native trick he had learned in Uganda. He slid down the tree. He caught hold of a springy young sapling and to it he fastened his hunting knife, with the blade pointing down the trail; with a bit of wild grapevine he tied back the sapling. Then he ran for his life. The hounds raised their voices as they hit the fresh scent. Rainsford knew now how an animal at bay feels.

He had to stop to get his breath. The baying of the hounds stopped abruptly, and Rainsford's heart stopped too. They must have reached the knife.

He shinned excitedly up a tree and looked back. His pursuers had stopped. But the hope that was in Rainsford's brain when he climbed died, for he saw in the shallow valley that General Zaroff was still on his feet. But Ivan was not. The knife, driven by the recoil of the springing tree, had not wholly failed.

Rainsford had hardly tumbled to the ground when the pack resumed the chase.

"Nerve, nerve, nerve!" he panted, as he dashed along. A blue gap showed between the trees dead ahead. Ever nearer drew the hounds. Rainsford forced himself on toward that gap. He reached it. It was the shore of the sea. Across a cove he could see the gloomy gray stone of the château. Twenty feet below him the sea rumbled and hissed. Rainsford hesitated. He heard the hounds. Then he leaped far out into the sea. . . .

When the general and his pack reached the place by the sea, the Cossack stopped. For some minutes he stood regarding the blue-green expanse of water. He shrugged his shoulders. Then he sat down, and hummed a bit from *Madame Butterfly*.

General Zaroff had an exceedingly good dinner in his great paneled dining hall that evening. With it he had a bottle of Pol Roger and a half bottle of Chambertin. Two slight annoyances kept him from perfect enjoyment. One was the thought that it would be difficult to replace Ivan; the other was that his quarry had escaped him. Of course, the American hadn't played the game — so thought the general as he tasted his after-dinner liqueur. In his library he read, to soothe himself, from the works of Marcus Aurelius. At ten he went up to his bedroom. He was deliciously tired, he said to himself, as he locked himself in. There was a little moonlight, so before turning on his light, he went to the window and looked down at the courtyard. To the great hounds he called: "Better luck another time!" Then he switched on the light.

A man, who had been hiding in the curtains of the bed, was standing there.

"Rainsford!" screamed the general. "How in God's name did you get here?"

"Swam," said Rainsford. "I found it quicker than walking through the jungle."

The general sucked in his breath and smiled. "I congratulate you," he said. "You have won the game."

Rainsford did not smile. "I am still a beast at bay," he said, in a low, hoarse voice. "Get ready, General Zaroff."

The general made one of his deepest bows. "I see," he said. "Splendid! One of us is to furnish a repast for the hounds. The other will sleep in this very excellent bed. On guard, Rainsford." . . .

He had never slept in a better bed, Rainsford decided.

Laughter and Light

Some writers say that the only difference between humour and tragedy is the outcome. It is true that we tend to laugh and cry over the same things. If a situation ends well, it can be viewed from the distance of time as funny, regardless of the mishaps along the way.

Charlie Chaplin played a tramp in the movie, *The Gold Rush*. A brilliant and wildly funny scene occurs in which the tramp eats a shoe. The great comedy team of Laurel and Hardy were always slipping on banana peels, falling off buildings into tubs of mud or cement, almost being run down by a fast train. Had the tramp died from starvation, or had Laurel and Hardy been hit by the train, the situation would have been tragic. The geniuses of comedy have always walked the thin edge between laughter and tears.

We need to be able to laugh at ourselves, to chuckle over our little faults and smile at our foolishness. People who can do this survive well through life.

Look upon these stories as friends who help you to get outside yourself. They are meant to give you a lighter view of the world. That's what this section is all about — LAUGHTER AND LIGHT.

The Harps of Heaven

John Durham

"What hit me?" Owen asked.
"A piano," Rainey said.

"**H**ow many dollars did you say?" Rainey's old man tilted his head to look at Mrs. Scott. He squinched up his left eye.

"I don't see how I can ask less than —"

"Half the ivory's off the keys," Rainey's old man said. "And it ain't tuned."

"Ain't tuned?" Mrs. Scott shuffled over and knocked out four bars of Walk Right in, Set Right Down. "That's tuned," she said.

"Hey, that's pretty good," Rainey said.

"Shut up," his old man said. "That song, nobody can't tell if it tuned or not. Thirty-five."

"I don't want no piano," Rainey said.

"Shut up," his old man said. "Nobody done asked you."

"Well, ask me," Rainey said, "and I'm going to tell you I don't want no piano."

"Hear that?" Rainey's father said to Mrs. Scott. "What's that sound like to you?"

"Sound like he don't want a piano. Sound like that," she said.

"No, that ain't what it sound like. No. What it sound like, it sound like a boy about to get warped. You want to get warped?" he said to Rainey.

"No," Rainey said, "but I don't want no piano, neither."

"If I hit him," Rainey's old man said, "I got to pay the doctor. That's the whole trouble."

"I don't see how I can ask less than for —," Mrs. Scott said.

"Thirty-five," Rainey's old man said. "And not one little old penny more."

"You got to move it," Mrs. Scott said.

"That's all right."

"Well," Mrs. Scott said. She folded her hands.

"Here's your thirty-five dollars," Rainey's old man said. "Three tens and a five. If you just write me out a receipt."

"How you going to get it over to your place?" Mrs. Scott said.

"I got me some boys out there in a pickup truck. That's how."

Mrs. Scott looked at him for a long time. "I just wish I had knowed that," she said. "That you wanted that piano that much."

Rainey's old man laughed. "I just bet you do," he said.

Mrs. Scott handed him the receipt. "Couple of things," she said.

"What's that?" Rainey's father said.

"Before I give that boy his first lesson."

"Yeah?" Rainey's father said.

"Tell him to wash his hands. That's one thing."

"Yeah? And what's the other?"

"You better have my husband come over with his tuning kit. Just to round off the edges. Charge ain't much."

"How much is not much?"

"Ten dollars," Mrs. Scott said. "Call any time."

On the way out, Rainey tossed up his baseball and caught it, five or six times. "I seen the piano," he said. "And I watched you get beat in the bargain. Now, can I go play some ball?"

"You cannot," his old man said.

"The guys are waiting for me. I got to pitch," Rainey said.

"You got to help Fats and Josh and me carry that piano — up three flights of stairs."

Rainey rode in the back of the pickup truck. He sat on the piano stool, leaning his elbows on the keys. He squeezed his baseball and thought dark thoughts about his old man. He wished his old man would remember when he was a boy. Did he want to play a beat-up piano? Or did he want to get out of the house and live?

Rainey pictured himself on the mound. He saw himself cool, eyeing the batter. The batter looked scared. And he ought to, with Big Rainey Dukes on the mound. He rolled up his hand in the mitt. He leaned way back, way, way back. And he threw it in there. The ball headed straight for the batter. The batter jumped back. The ball broke neatly and dipped in across the plate. Strike! Yeah! Yeah! Strike! And another one coming up. Oh, baseball was the thing. A person could squeeze that ball in his hand and feel good. He could smell the horsehide. He could smell his own good sweat. Baseball, that sport made him feel like somebody. It did.

"Now you get up here at the top and like guide it," his father said. They had pushed the piano up across the open courtyard. Now they were going up the stairs. "You get up at the top, Rainey. And Fats will help you. Me and Josh will push from down here."

It went all right up to the first landing. There was a little problem about turning the piano around the corner. But it went all right up the second floor even.

"That thing's not heavy as she looks," Josh said. He sat next to Rainey's old man, on the top stair. "She ain't so heavy."

"She's heavy enough," Fats said. He was lying on the floor, next to Rainey. He just about got the words out, between puffs and gasps for breath.

"Let's go," Rainey's old man said. He stood up.

"Go?" Fats said.

"Push that there piano on up them stairs," said Rainey's old man.

"We going to go," Fats said, still on the floor. "We might as well go straight on to the funeral parlor."

"You'll make it," Rainey's old man said. He held out his hand to Fats and pulled him up.

"Who got me into this?" Fats said. "I got some eight-ball to shoot."

"Come on," Rainey's old man said. "You get up at the top again."

It didn't go so well that time. Just before they got the piano to the first landing, something cracked and groaned. It was way down inside the piano, whatever it was.

"Stop," Rainey's old man said. "What's that?"

"That's my insides," Fats said.

Rainey thought that was pretty funny. He was bitter. He knew the whole team was waiting for him over at the park. But he thought that was funny. He laughed that high, horsey laugh of his.

"Your wife have this kid?" Fats said. "Or did you get traded for him at a stable?"

That made Rainey laugh even harder. Stable!

"Somebody got cheated," Fats said. "And it wasn't the other guy."

"Let's take it on up," Josh said. "My arms are quivering and trembling."

"You think she'll break?" Rainey's old man said.

"If she don't, I will," Josh said. "Let's go, man." He sounded sort of desperate.

They got to the second-floor landing. Fats fell backwards onto the floor with a loud grunt. Josh slumped down on a stair and leaned against the railing. Even Rainey's old man was pooped.

"Can I go play ball when we get her up?" Rainey said.

"Play ball?" Josh said. "You going to go out from here and lift a baseball? A big old, heavy baseball? They going to have to carry me down these here stairs."

"You got all that much energy," Rainey's old man said. "You just get down on the bottom with me and let old Josh help Fats."

"He can't help me," Fats said. "There ain't no help for me. I died five minutes ago."

It was slow work up to the half-way landing on the third flight. The piano was too big to sit there all by itself. So they let her hang half-way out in the air. Fats collapsed across the top of the one end to hold her. Rainey leaned against the wall and looked out the big window that went from the floor almost to the ceiling. Down in the court he could see somebody waving up to him. Who was it?

"Who's that?" his old man said. "And what's he got? Saint Vitus dance?"

"It's Owney Watson," said Rainey.

"What's he want?"

"Me to come pitch."

"I hear one more word about baseball, I'm going to keep you locked up in the house. Playing this here piano."

Rainey thought about that when they were half-way up the next flight. He knew his old man was just talking. He knew that. He also knew that he, Rainey, would spend hours next to Mrs. Scott banging on this thing. Hours, every week. Hours away from the baseball diamond.

They were just about to the top when the trouble hit Rainey's old man. "Lord God in Heaven," he shouted. "Stop, stop, stop!"

Fats looked down the top of the piano at him. "What's got you, man?" he said.

"My back," Rainey's old man said. "Oh, oh, my back." He said some other very colorful words. He said them loud and clear. He let go the piano with one hand and clutched the small of his back.

"It's slipping!" Rainey said. "I can't hold it."

"Come down here, Fats," groaned Rainey's old man. "Come get this thing."

"How was I supposed to come?" Fats said. The piano was blocking the stairs. "I ain't learned to really fly yet. I'm only on the third lesson."

That did it for Rainey, that joke. It caught him down in the gut. He started in on one of those high, horsey belly laughs. And that got Fats to whooping and groaning. Josh was too far gone. He leaned on the top of the piano and stared from one to the other. His eyes were as glassy as marbles.

"Oh, you laugh away," Rainey's old man said. "I'm dying here, and you two got to laugh. My back straightens up and I kill both of you!"

The piano groaned, deep down inside. Little jingly tunes sounded in the middle of the groans, little sad tunes. It slipped down the second step, a little faster.

"She's going!" Josh yelled. "She's going!"

"Thanks for telling me," Rainey's old man said. "Thirty-five dollars," he said. He said some more colorful words.

The piano, going a little faster now, went down another step and another.

"Man, you going to get mashed." Josh yelled.

"I can't hardly move."

"You better move," Josh said.

"They ain't no place to go."

"Come up across the top," Josh yelled. "Quick! She's heading for the window!"

Rainey didn't know how he did it. Nobody could do it. But he picked up his old man and threw him across the top of the piano — right before he mounted the top himself. The piano was going pretty fast, down the last three or four stairs. It was moving now, and the songs it sang were quicker. They sounded almost happy. Not that Rainey cared. He was waltzing across the top of the piano, but he didn't think he needed any music. All he needed was to get his feet back on the floor — get back on the floor before the piano sailed out the big window, three floors up.

He hit the air just when the piano hit the glass. There was a big crash — glass, broken wood, loudly jangling piano. Rainey turned in mid-air. He could see it all at once. He could see Fats and Josh sitting on the stairs with their mouths open. He could see his old man, clutching his back and his forehead at the same time. "Thirty-five dollars," his old man was saying. He sounded as if he could cry.

At the same time, up there in mid-air, Rainey could see the piano. It hung over the courtyard. Just hung there in mid-air, with pieces of glass in the air all around it. It was playing little songs again, like the harps of heaven. Next to it, up against the blue sky, there was a pigeon, looking troubled.

Then the piano was gone. There it was, piano, pigeon, little jingling songs. Then it was all gone at once. In its place there was the loudest musical noise Rainey ever heard. It rose to the skies, the last song Mrs. Scott's piano would ever play. One deep chord sounded, cement, wood, piano strings. And one human voice. That was when Rainey remembered old Owney Watson.

He thought about Owney just when his feet hit the floor. He could almost cry. Old Owney was the best catcher in town, no doubt about that. Rainey hated to think he had been mashed by a secondhand piano. He thought about Owney all the way down the stairs. Fats and Josh and his old man were right behind him. He thought about Owney and how his team was just sure to lose the game without him. Nobody could call a pitch like old Owney.

Owney looked a little strange lying there. He looked a little odd with the piano wire wrapped around him and the piano keys scattered like dominoes over his chest. He looked slightly kinky with the pigeon sitting on his forehead. But his eyes were open.

"You all right?" Rainey asked.

"What hit me?" Owney asked.

"A piano," Rainey said.

"I guess so."

"Can you play?" Rainey asked.

"Sure. If you take that pigeon out of my eyes."

Rainey picked up the pigeon. It still looked troubled. It looked worried and upset. It was a pale blue pigeon with little shiny scarlet eyes and red feet. It didn't look hurt, just worried.

People came out of doors all over the place. They gathered around Rainey and the pigeon and Owney and the gutted piano. Over them all hung the piano's last song, echoing from the walls of the courtyard. It was almost solemn, almost sad.

"Maybe it wasn't much of a piano," Fats said finally. "But it did something no other piano ever did."

"What's that?" Josh asked.

"Got a pigeon on the wing," Fats said. "Not many pianos can make that statement."

"No," Josh said to Rainey's old man, "and it's going to save you money on tuning."

"Where you going?" Rainey's old man said to Rainey.

"Over to the ball park," Rainey said. "I got me a game to pitch."

"You come back here," Rainey's old man said. "Go on and pitch. I just want me something out of this deal. That's all."

"What you want?" Rainey said.

"Give me that pigeon there," Rainey's old man said. "It ain't much. A little old pigeon. Oh, it ain't much. But it's something."

"What you going to do with him?" Fats asked.

"Do? I ain't going to do nothing. I'm going to set, that's all, and think how a man goes through a day. He starts out with thirty-five dollars in his pocket."

"Yeah," Fats said, "and we all know how he ends up."

"We do," Rainey's old man said. "With a handful of feathers."

In the Long Run

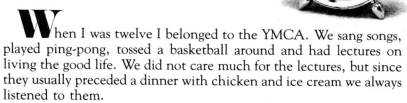

Robert Fontaine

"No one suspected that when a detective opened his locker in the YMCA one night he would find seven track suits, nine pairs of basketball kneepads, four pairs of sneakers . . . ."

When I was twelve I belonged to the YMCA. We sang songs, played ping-pong, tossed a basketball around and had lectures on living the good life. We did not care much for the lectures, but since they usually preceded a dinner with chicken and ice cream we always listened to them.

I used to wonder how my cousin Roy could do it. Roy was a collector of anything he saw lying around. He explained that his father was sick, his mother worked for less than nothing and the only way he could survive was to pick up a bit here and there.

Of course I could not agree with his theory, even if at times I admired his cunning and nerve. The point is that I was astonished at the way Roy could listen without blinking to all the lectures and then go right ahead and operate.

We would come from the lecture and Roy would take two chocolate bars from the supervisor's desk. Then he would put twenty-five cents in the cashbox and remove change for a dollar.

"I don't count very good," Roy explained whenever I caught him.

He was a good-looking, husky boy with dark hair, laughing eyes and strong white teeth. He looked young and innocent and no one suspected that when a detective opened his locker in the YMCA one night he would find seven track suits, nine pairs of basketball kneepads, four pairs of sneakers and a dozen other items. It was marvelous how Roy could get all the stuff in his locker, let alone the manner in which he acquired it.

The truth, which Roy told me once, was that he went around to all the lockers, row after row, and twisted the combinations this way and that way. Sometimes, some of the lockers opened. Roy would take one or two garments and lock up again. All the things were too big for him and he never sold them. I do not know why he picked them up. But he did.

Anyway, the detective took him up to the supervisor's office and he asked me to come along, too. I believe they suspected I was an accomplice, but I was as blameless as a baby.

We sat down on hard chairs and watched the gold desk clock ticking and listened to our hearts beating. I was very nervous, this being the first time I was ever involved in a larceny. Mr. Wakes, the boys' supervisor, was a gentle, pale-eyed man with a sharp nose and little hair. He paced around us for a time in silence. Then he said to me:

"What do you know about this?"

"Nothing, sir."

"Did you know your cousin was taking this — these — taking —"

"No, sir."

"Hmm." He turned to Roy who smiled at him so pleasantly that it was apparently difficult to find the words.

"Roy," he began, "you are one of the most active boys in this Y. You are a fine athlete. You have a good personality. When there is work to be done you do much more than your share. Tell me, why do you steal?"

"I don't steal," Roy said. At this, the detective sat up and blinked.

"How's that?" he asked sharply.

"You heard me," Roy said. "And we don't smoke in the boys' department. We don't like to encourage it. Isn't that right, Mr. Wakes?"

Mr. Wakes smiled for a moment, rather pleased. "Yes, yes, Roy. Exactly." He turned to the detective. "You understand?"

The detective squashed out his cigar in the ash tray by the gold clock.

"Also we remove our hats immediately upon entering the department," Roy said. The detective looked daggers at Mr. Wakes, but he took off his hat.

"Listen," the detective said, "this kid is a thief. What are we standing here for, talking?"

"He said he didn't steal anything," Mr. Wakes said vaguely. "We — uh — we — can't judge the boy without giving him a hearing."

"Listen," the detective said to Roy. "Confess. Go straight. You'll get off with a suspended sentence in reform school."

"I have nothing to confess," Roy said.

The detective raised his hand as if to wallop Roy, but Mr. Wakes stopped him, gently. "Let us be — uh — uh — gentlemen about this."

"Look," the detective said, "I opened his locker. I saw the stuff lying there. I got a list of the stolen property. The stolen property was in his locker. It's an open-and-shut case."

"Nobody has preferred any charges yet," Roy said.

"What does that mean?" I asked him in a whisper.

"No whispering!" the detective shouted.

"In the boys' department we are polite to each other. We do not shout nor use bad English. We respect each other," Roy said.

The detective turned to Mr. Wakes who was swallowing a little nervously. "Listen, brother. You asked for a detective. You said property was disappearing. Now we have done our duty and discovered the criminal. Let us go down and prefer charges."

"Uh —," Mr. Wakes said weakly, "we must be sure."

"Holy Moses! . . . The stuff was all there in the kid's locker," the detective shouted.

"In the boys' department we do not use profanity," Roy said. Mr. Wakes smiled, glad to be back in his element a moment. "Yes," he agreed, "we discourage even circumlocutions."

"Look," said the detective, very exasperated, "I am not here for a lecture. I am here to make a pinch. The stuff was found in the kid's locker —"

Mr. Wakes sighed and waved his hand ineffectually.

"It's not my locker," Roy said calmly. The detective blinked. Mr. Wakes opened his eyes wide. I nearly fainted.

"Whose locker is it then, little man?" the detective said sharply.

"His," Roy replied, pointing to me.

"But I don't use it," I said. "I hardly ever use it."

"Yes, come to think of it, the boys have been doubling up on the lockers," Mr. Wakes said. "This other young man is the soul of honor so I clear him instinctively. On the other hand, it is not Roy's locker. So the evidence, circumstantial as it is, cannot be used against Roy."

"Then who put the stuff in the locker?" the detective asked, running his hand over his hot face.

"I do not know," Roy said.

"Well, I'll be a monkey's uncle!" the detective declared.

"In the boys' department," Roy observed, "we are kind to animals."

The detective put on his hat, lit a cigar and went out, slamming the door. There was a long silence while Mr. Wakes looked out the window. In time he turned around and looked at us gently and a little wearily.

"Uh, boys—boys. I appoint you two boys to see that the stealing of —uh—garments, etc., is stopped. I have faith in you and I know you will apprehend the culprit and punish him in a proper fashion. Uh— I might add that crime does not pay. The man who begins in a small way ends up stealing large sums and is soon miserable."

"My uncle Joe stole ten thousand dollars from a bank and they haven't caught him yet," Roy said. "That was ten years ago. Every month or so we get a postcard from him in the Fiji Islands."

Mr. Wakes cleared his throat. "In the long run. In the long run, crime does not pay. The proof is that people at heart are honest. People are — uh — really good —"

"I know some awful stinkers," Roy said.

"Me, too," I agreed. Mr. Wakes sighed. "Yes, yes. But there is a trend toward goodness. In the long run we will all be good. Those of us who are bad must be considered ill. We must treat them for a disease of evil . . . and then one glorious day we shall all be well — and — uh, happy. In the long run. That is all, gentlemen."

We walked out slowly and down the stairs and toward the square. Roy was very solemn. After a while he spoke thoughtfully.

"You know, I feel bad for the first time in my life. Not because I stole the gym suits. They're no good anyway. I just didn't like all those senior guys shoving me around. I showed them it ain't enough to be big. You have to be smart, too. But something else. I mean I did something wrong.

"I talked about this old guy Wakes like he was crazy. But what happens? He knows I am poor so when I am not looking he puts a ten-dollar bill in my pocket. It makes me feel worse than stealing."

"I know," I said, as Roy reached in and took a ten-dollar bill from one pocket.

"I think I know what I'll do," he said, reaching into the other pocket, removing from it a shiny gold object. "I'll go back when he isn't looking and put back his clock."

In the long run, however, Roy came out all right. He became one of the city's finest detectives, although I have no idea how.

The Hitch-Hiker

Gregory Clark

"An Interesting Character is always a welcome pick-up. And sometimes you catch the top bracket of hitch-hikers, who are Philosophers."

The old boy on the side of the road, thumbing, was possibly a Character. Maybe even a Philosopher.

As a rule, I don't pick up hitch-hikers any more, unless they are in uniform. The last few times I have had fleas, it was due to having picked up Characters.

But this old boy, as I rapidly approached him, had an Interesting look. He might well be an Interesting Character. And when, at about forty yards, I detected at his feet a nice, clean, fresh-looking haversack, and when I perceived he had a fine, red, tanned face, and that his wispy white hair blowing in the wind could hardly be sticky, I threw overboard my prejudices and began to slacken speed. An Interesting Character is always a welcome pick-up. And sometimes you catch the top bracket of hitch-hikers, who are Philosophers.

"Hi!" I called out the window, noting with delight that he was carrying a gnarled walking stick.

He opened the door and lifted in his haversack.

In his wind-blown old face he had bright, sharp eyes, and all the wrinkles about them were from good nature.

Slowly he reached out and closed the door, glancing behind.

"Careful," he said. "Cars coming."

"I'll be careful," I assured him cheerily. "You've picked a careful driver."

"That I noticed," he said, "when I seen you coming in the distance."

"Aha! You pick your cars, eh?"

He was still turned to watch rearward.

"Yes, sir," he agreed. "I avoid these new-model cars."

"Well, heck," I protested. "This one isn't so ancient."

"It's O.K. now," said the old boy. "Nothing coming."

So I steered back off the shoulder and stepped on the gas. He continued to watch back.

"You're not nervous, are you?" I inquired, to get the ball rolling. "You can't be a hitch-hiker and nervous."

"No, sir, I ain't nervous," he said, turning and making himself comfortable. "And I am a regular, you might say a practising, hitch-hiker."

I knew I had a Philosopher.

"Well, sir," I said, "how far am I to have the pleasure of your company?"

"To Porter's Corners, if you're going that far," he replied. "Twenty-six miles. You come over a rise, and there's a big swamp spread out below —"

"I know it well," I assured him.

"Full of rabbits," he said. "Cottontail and swamp hare, both. AND foxes."

"I don't doubt that," I said.

A car whipped past us from behind, and the driver and the woman beside him both glared at us.

Indeed, they turned to glare back, after they had passed.

"What's eating them?" I put in.

"Oh, it's hard to say," said my Philosopher. "No accounting for manners on the highway, is there?"

Another car overtook us and swished past. The driver turned and motioned with his thumb, backwards.

"What's the matter with him?" I snorted.

"Guess he wants you to speed up," suggested the Philosopher.

"I'm hitting fifty," I stated. "That's my speed. And also the law's."

"They're always in a rush," admitted the old boy, turning to glance behind. "Nobody behind you. You ain't forming a line."

"I agree," I said, "that people who dawdle on the highway are the cause of more accidents than anybody else. A person going forty is bound to build up a tail of half a dozen or a dozen cars behind him. And trying to pass him results in more accidents than all the speed in the world. But tell me. About foxes. What is your interest in foxes and the big swamp at Porter's Corners? Are you a sportsman?"

"Well, no," said my kindly old passenger. "I guess I am what you might call a naturalist or something. I just like to set in the swamp and look and listen."

"Well, now!" I exclaimed, delighted. "Orchids? Birds?"

"Yes and no," said my Philosopher. "They're all part of it. Just setting and listening and watching."

"You a farmer?"

"No, I spent my life as a sawmill hand," said the old boy. "But I been retired now twenty years or so. Living on my daughter, a fine woman."

"You interest me," I declared. "How about this business of sitting in a swamp, looking and listening? Tell me about this."

Two cars from behind overtook us and sped past. The first was driven by a man who had three women passengers. They all glared back at me, and waved their hands in a menacing fashion. The second car was full of small children in the rear window, and they, wide-eyed, waved and yelled and pressed their noses against the glass.

"For goodness' sake," I announced, looking at my speedometer.

"This craze for speed," said my companion.

So I put on five miles and brought her up to fifty-five.

"Not that fast," cautioned my Philosopher, taking a gander out the back window as I accelerated.

But I held it at fifty-five, as we chatted about swamps and orchids and screech owls and foxes; and presently we overtook a thin-necked gentleman with large ears going about forty.

"Look at this," I pointed out to my passenger. "Dawdling along at his own sweet pace."

We swished past him.

In a moment, I became aware that the dawdling gentleman was right on my tail. He moved out to pass.

"Just look at that!" I cried. "We pass him and right away —"

The dawdler shot past me. And hardly had he passed me before he began to slacken speed.

"Why, the son of a gun!" I gritted. "Imagine that! Going forty or less, and now —"

I veered out and leaped past him. He gave a couple of toots on his horn, put on speed, passed me, and hardly had he passed before he again slackened speed so that I nearly ran him down.

"One of these here traffic evangelists," commented my Philosopher, "trying to teach others how to drive, eh?"

I veered out and passed him, and as I did so I turned to give him an indignant glare. He was motioning energetically toward the back of my car.

I drew over to the shoulder. He pulled up behind me.

I got out.

"You got a dog," he called from his window, "on your back bumper!"

Sure enough, there was a hound squatted cosily on my back bumper, slapping his tail.

"Well," explained my old Philosopher, as he bailed out. "Nobody will pick me up with a hound. So I trained him to hide in the bushes, and jump on whenever I get aboard."

"Old-model cars — ," I reflected.

"I pick 'em," said he, "for their big bumpers. I know my models."

The hound's name was Bojangles. We took him in the car. A fine, wise Redbone he was. And I let the Philosopher and Bojangles out at their favourite entry to the Porter's Corners swamp.

And I wished to God I could have gone with them.

The Dentist and the Gas

Stephen Leacock

Of course I didn't *feel* it. All I felt was that someone dealt me a powerful blow in the face with a sledge-hammer.

"I think," said the dentist, stepping outside again, "I'd better give you gas."

Then he moved aside and hummed an air from a light opera, while he mixed up cement.

I sat up in my shroud.

"Gas!" I said.

"Yes," he repeated, "gas or else ether or a sulphuric anesthetic or else beat you into insensibility with a club or give you three thousand volts of electricity."

These may not have been his exact words. But they convey the feeling of them very nicely.

I could see the light of primitive criminality shining behind the man's spectacles.

And to think that this was *my* fault — the result of my own reckless neglect. I had grown so used to sitting back dozing in my shroud in the dentist's chair, listening to the twittering of the birds outside, my eyes closed in the sweet half sleep of perfect security, that the old apprehensiveness and mental agony had practically all gone.

He didn't hurt me, and I knew it.

I had grown — I know it sounds mad — almost to like him.

For a time I had kept up the appearance of being hurt every few minutes, just as a precaution. Then even that had ceased, and I had dropped into vainglorious apathy.

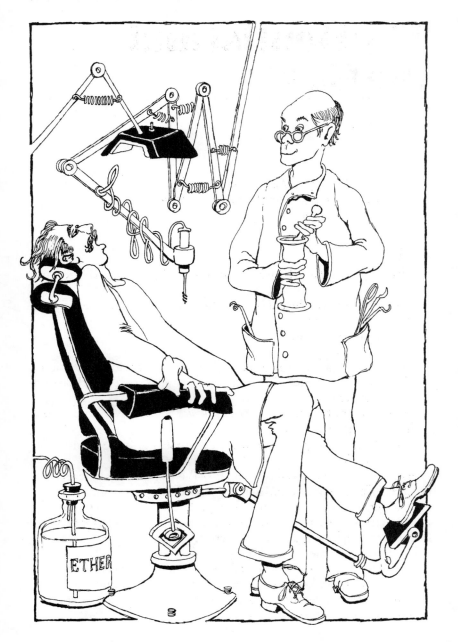

It was this, of course, which had infuriated the dentist. He meant to reassert his power. He knew that nothing but gas could rouse me out of my lethargy and he meant to apply it — either gas or some other powerful pain stimulant.

So as soon as he said *gas*, my senses were alert in a moment.

"When are you going to do it?" I said in horror.

"Right now, if you like," he answered.

His eyes were glittering with what the Germans call Blutlust. All dentists have it.

I could see that if I took my eye off him for a moment he might spring at me, gas in hand, and throttle me.

"No, not now, I can't stay now," I said, "I have an appointment, a whole lot of appointments, urgent ones, the most urgent I ever had." I was unfastening my shroud as I spoke.

"Well then, to-morrow," said the dentist.

"No," I said, "to-morrow is Saturday. And Saturday is a day when I simply can't take gas. If I take gas, even the least bit of gas, on a Saturday, I find it's misunderstood."

"Monday, then."

"Monday, I'm afraid, won't do. It's a bad day for me, worse than I can explain."

"Tuesday?" said the dentist.

"Not Tuesday," I answered, "Tuesday is the worst day of all. On Tuesday my church society meets, and I *must* go to it."

I hadn't been near it in reality for three years, but suddenly I felt a longing to attend it.

"On Wednesday," I went on, speaking hurriedly and wildly, "I have another appointment, a swimming club, and on Thursday two appointments, a choral society and a funeral. On Friday I have another funeral. Saturday is market day. Sunday is washing day. Monday is drying day —"

"Hold on," said the dentist, speaking very firmly. "You come to-morrow morning, I'll write the engagement for ten o'clock."

I think it must have been hypnotism.

Before I knew it, I had said "Yes."

I went out.

In the street, I met a man I knew.

"Have you ever taken gas from a dentist?" I asked.

"Oh, yes," he said. "It's nothing."

Soon after I met another man.

"Have you ever taken gas?" I asked.

"Oh, certainly," he answered, "it's nothing, nothing at all."

Altogether I asked about fifty people that day about gas and they all said that it was absolutely nothing. When I said that I was to take it to-morrow, they showed no concern whatever. I looked in their faces for traces of anxiety. There weren't any. They all said that it wouldn't hurt me, that it was nothing.

So then I was glad because I knew that gas was nothing.

It began to seem hardly worth while to keep the appointment. Why go all the way down town for such a mere nothing?

But I did go.

I kept the appointment.

What followed was such an absolute nothing that I shouldn't bother to relate it except for the sake of my friends.

The dentist was there with two assistants. All three had white coats on, as rigid as naval uniforms.

I forget whether they carried revolvers.

Nothing could exceed their quiet courage. Let me pay them that tribute.

I was laid out in my shroud in a long chair and tied down to it — I think I was tied down; perhaps I was fastened with nails — this part of it was a mere nothing. It simply felt like being tied down by three strong men armed with pinchers.

After that a gas tank and a pump were placed beside me and a set of rubber tubes fastened tight over my mouth and nose. Even those who have never taken gas can realise how ridiculously simple is this.

Then they began pumping in gas. The sensation of this part of it I cannot, unfortunately, recall. It happened that just as they began to administer the gas, I fell asleep. I don't quite know why. Perhaps I was overtired. Perhaps it was the simple home charm of the surroundings, the soft drowsy hum of the gas pump, the twittering of the dentists in the trees — did I say in the trees? — No, of course they weren't in the trees — imagine dentists in the trees! — ha! ha! — here, take off this gas pipe from my face till I laugh — really I just want to laugh — only to laugh —

Well, that's what it felt like.

Meanwhile, they were operating.

Of course I didn't *feel* it. All I felt was that someone dealt me a powerful blow in the face with a sledge-hammer. After that somebody took a pick-axe and cracked in my jaw with it. That was all.

It was a mere nothing. I felt at the time that a man who objects to a few taps on the face with a pick-axe is over-critical.

I didn't happen to wake up till they had practically finished. So I really missed the whole thing.

The assistants had gone and the dentist was mixing up cement and humming airs from light opera just like old times. It made the world seem a bright place.

I went home with no teeth. I only meant them to remove one, but I realised that they had taken them all out. Still, it didn't matter.

Not long after I received my bill. I was astounded at the nerve of it; for administering gas, so much; for removing teeth, so much — and so on.

In return I sent in my bill:

DR. WILLIAM JAWS

To mental agony	$ 50.00
To gross lies in regard to the nothingness of gas	100.00
To putting me under gas	50.00
To having fun with me under gas	100.00
To Brilliant Ideas, occurred to me under gas and lost	100.00
Grand Total	$400.00

My bill has been contested and is in the hands of a solicitor. The matter will prove, I understand, a test case, and will go to the final courts. If the judges have toothache during the trial, I shall win.

A Genuine Mexican Plug

Mark Twain

He came down, and immediately hoisted his heels into the air, delivering a vicious kick on the sky, and stood on his fore feet.

I resolved to have a horse to ride. I had never seen such wild, free, magnificent horsemanship outside of a circus as these picturesquely-clad Mexicans, Californians, and Mexicanized Americans displayed in Carson streets every day. How they rode! Leaning just gently forward, easy and nonchalant, with broad slouch-hat brim blown square up in front, and long riata swinging above the head, they swept through the town like the wind! The next minute they were only a sailing puff of dust on the far desert. If they trotted, they sat up gallantly and gracefully, and seemed part of the horse; did not go jiggering up and down after the silly fashion of the riding-schools. I had quickly learned to tell a horse from a cow, and was full of anxiety to learn more. I was resolved to buy a horse.

While the thought was rankling in my mind, the auctioneer came scurrying through the plaza on a black beast that had as many humps and corners on him as a dromedary, and was necessarily uncomely; but he was "going, going, at twenty-two! — horse, saddle and bridle at twenty-two dollars, gentlemen!" and I could hardly resist.

A man whom I did not know (he turned out to be the auctioneer's brother) noticed the wistful look in my eye, and observed that that was a very remarkable horse to be going at such a price; and added that the saddle alone was worth the money. It was a Spanish saddle, with ponderous tapidaros, and furnished with the ungainly sole-leather covering with the unspellable name. I said I had half a notion to bid. Then this keen-eyed person appeared to me to be "taking my measure"; but I dismissed the suspicion when he spoke, for his manner was full of guileless candor and truthfulness. Said he:

"I know that horse — know him well. You are a stranger, I take it, and so you might think he was an American horse, maybe, but I assure you he is not. He is nothing of the kind; but—excuse my speaking in a low voice, other people being near — he is, without the shadow of a doubt, a Genuine Mexican Plug!"

I did not know what a Genuine Mexican Plug was, but there was something about this man's way of saying it, that made me swear inwardly that I would own a Genuine Mexican Plug, or die.

"Has he any other—er—advantages?" I inquired, suppressing what eagerness I could.

He hooked his forefinger in the pocket of my army-shirt, led me to one side, and breathed in my ear impressively these words:

"He can out-buck anything in America!"

"Going, going, going — twenty-ty-four dollars and a half, gen—"

"Twenty-seven!" I shouted in a frenzy.

"And sold!" said the auctioneer, and passed over the Genuine Mexican Plug to me.

I could scarcely contain my exultation. I paid the money, and put the animal in a neighboring livery-stable to dine and rest himself.

In the afternoon I brought the creature into the plaza, and certain citizens held him by the head, and others by the tail, while I mounted him. As soon as they let go, he placed all his feet in a bunch together, lowered his back, and then suddenly arched it upward and shot me straight into the air a matter of three or four feet! I came as straight down again, lit in the saddle, went instantly up again, came down almost on the high pommel, shot up again, and came down on the horse's neck — all in the space of three or four seconds. Then he rose and stood almost straight up on his hind feet, and I, clasping his lean neck desperately, slid back into the saddle, and held on. He came down, and immediately hoisted his heels into the air, delivering a vicious kick on the sky, and stood on his fore feet. And then down he came once more, and began the original exercise of shooting me straight up again.

The third time I heard a stranger say: "Oh, don't he buck, though!"

While I was up, somebody struck the horse a sounding thwack with a leathern strap, and when I arrived down again the Genuine Mexican Plug was not there. A Californian youth chased him up and caught him, and asked if he might have a ride. I granted him that luxury. He mounted the Genuine, got lifted into the air once, but sent his spurs home as he descended, and the horse darted away like a telegram. He soared over three fences like a bird, and disappeared down the road toward the Washoe Valley.

I sat down on a stone with a sigh, and by natural impulse one of my hands sought my forehead, and the other the base of my stomach. I believe I never appreciated, till then, the poverty of the human machinery — for I still needed a hand or two to place elsewhere. Pen cannot describe how I was jolted up. Imagination cannot conceive how disjointed I was — how internally, externally, and universally I was unsettled, mixed up, and ruptured. There was a sympathetic crowd around me though.

One elderly-looking comforter said:

"Stranger, you've been taken in. Everybody in this camp knows that horse. Any child could have told you that he'd buck; he is the very worst devil to buck on the continent of America. You hear me. I'm Curry. Old Curry. Old Abe Curry. And moreover, he is a simon-pure, out-and-out genuine d***d Mexican plug, and an uncommon mean one at that, too. Why, you turnip, if you had laid low and kept dark, there's chances to buy a good horse for mighty little more than you paid for that bloody old relic."

I gave no sign; but I made up my mind that if the auctioneer's brother's funeral took place while I was in the Territory I would postpone all other recreations and attend it.

After a gallop of sixteen miles, the California youth and the Genuine Mexican Plug came tearing into town again, shedding foam-flakes like the spume-spray that drives before a typhoon, and, with one final skip over a wheelbarrow, cast anchor in front of the "ranch".

Such panting and blowing! Such spreading and contracting of the red equine nostrils, and glaring of the wild equine eye! But was the imperial beast subjugated? Indeed, he was not. His lordship the Speaker of the House thought he was, and mounted him to go down to the Capitol; but the first dash the creature made was over a pile of telegraph poles half as high as a church; and his time to the Capitol — one mile and three-quarters — remains unbeaten to this day. But then he took an advantage — he left out the mile, and only did the three-quarters. That is to say, he made a straight cut across lots, preferring fences and ditches to a crooked road; and when the Speaker got to the Capitol he said he had been in the air so much he felt as if he had made the trip on a comet.

In the evening the Speaker came home afoot for exercise, and got the Genuine towed back behind a quartz wagon. The next day I loaned the animal to the Clerk of the House to go down to the Dana silver mine, six miles, and he walked back for exercise, and got the horse towed. Everybody I loaned him to always walked back; they never could get enough exercise any other way. Still, I continued to loan him to anybody who was willing to borrow him, my idea being to get him crippled, and throw him on the borrower's hands, or killed, and make the borrower pay for him. But somehow nothing ever happened to him. He took chances that no other horse ever took and survived, but he always came out safe. It was his daily habit to try experiments that had always before been considered impossible, but he always got through. Sometimes he miscalculated a little, and did not get his rider through intact, but he always got through himself. Of course I had tried to sell him; but that was a stretch of simplicity which met with little sympathy. The auctioneer stormed up and down the streets on him for four days, dispersing the populace, interrupting business, and destroying children, and never got a bid—at least never any but the eighteen-dollar one he hired a notoriously substanceless bummer to make. The people only smiled pleasantly, and restrained their desire to buy, if they had any. Then the auctioneer brought in his bill, and I withdrew the horse from the market. We tried to trade him off at private vendue next, offering him at a sacrifice for second-hand tombstones, old iron, temperance tracts — any kind of property. But holders were still, and we retired from the market again. I never tried to ride the horse any more. Walking was good enough exercise for a man like me, that had nothing the matter with him except ruptures, internal injuries, and such things. Finally I tried to give him away. But it was a failure. Parties said earthquakes were handy enough on the Pacific coast—they did not wish to own one. As a last resort I offered him to the Governor for the use of the "Brigade". His face lit up eagerly at first, but toned down again, and he said the thing would be too palpable.

Just then the livery stable man brought in his bill for six weeks' keeping—stall-room for the horse, fifteen dollars; hay for the horse, two hundred and fifty! The Genuine Mexican Plug had eaten a ton of the article, and the man said he would have eaten a hundred if he had let him.

I will remark here, in all seriousness, that the regular price of hay during that year and a part of the next was really two hundred and fifty dollars a ton, in gold, and during the winter before that there was such scarcity of the article that in several instances small quantities had brought eight hundred dollars a ton in coin! The consequence might be guessed without my telling it: people turned their stock loose to starve, and before the spring arrived Carson and Eagle Valleys were almost literally carpeted with their carcasses! Any old settler there will verify these statements.

I managed to pay the livery bill, and the same day I gave the Genuine Mexican Plug to a passing Arkansas emigrant whom fortune delivered into my hand. If this ever meets his eye, he will doubtless remember the donation.

Now whoever has the luck to ride a real Mexican plug will recognize the animal depicted in this chapter, and hardly consider him exaggerated—but the uninitiated will feel justified in regarding his portrait as a fancy sketch, perhaps.

The Unexplained and Unexplored

Our lives are changing faster than the life of anyone who has ever lived. Inventions by the hundred appear in the marketplace each year. Probes to other planets occur often enough to have them mentioned only in the back pages of the newspaper. Messages will soon be sent through the earth's centre to other parts of the world. And we have developed the power to build a paradise or wreck the planet.

What do fiction writers have to do with all this? It seems uncanny, but most of what we accept as fact today was fiction yesterday. The writer, not the scientist, was often first on the scene. Jules Verne first described an atomic submarine in the 19th century and called it the *Nautilus*. The first atomic submarine commissioned by the United States in 1952 was christened *Nautilus*. H. G. Wells, another "pre-atomic" writer, described a journey to the moon and back. He also described the invasion of earth by aliens. Old comic strip serials predicted the future, too: *Buck Rogers*, a comic strip of the 30's and 40's, included the jet-pak, a device worn on the back for easy manoeuvring over land and through space. It has since been developed. *Dick Tracy*, another comic strip of the same era, had its characters using tiny wrist radios before anyone had even dreamed of building transistors.

The unexplained and the unexplored are challenging and fun to think about. Some of the stories in this section may be predictions of things to come; other stories are pure fantasy to give our minds a holiday. Whether it is the challenge of the future or the pleasure of the fantasy, welcome to the galaxy of the imagination.

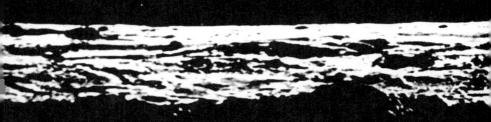

Test

Theodore Thomas

The car turned sideways. It was then his
mother began to scream.

Robert Proctor was a good driver for so young a person. The
turnpike curved gently ahead of him. Travel was light on this cool
morning in May. He felt rested, but alert. He had been driving for two
hours.

The sun was bright but not glaring. The air smelled fresh and clean.
He breathed in deeply. It was a good day for driving.

He looked at the gray-haired woman sitting in the front seat with
him. Her mouth was curved in a quiet smile. As she watched the trees
and fields slip by on her side of the turnpike Robert Proctor looked
back at the road. "Enjoying it, Mom?" he asked.

"Yes, Robert." Her voice was as cool as the morning.

He listened to the smooth purr of the engine. Up ahead he saw a big
truck. It was spouting smoke as it sped along the turnpike. Behind it
was a blue convertible, content to stay in line.

Robert Proctor noted this and put it in the back of his mind. He was
slowly overtaking the car and the truck. He would reach them in
another minute or two.

It was a good morning for driving. He pulled up and began to pass
the blue convertible. Though his speed was a few miles an hour above
the turnpike limit, his car was under perfect control.

The blue convertible suddenly swung out from behind the truck without warning. It struck his car near the right front fender. His car was knocked to the shoulder next to the turnpike median strip.

Robert Proctor was too wise to slam on the brakes. He fought the steering wheel to hold the car on a straight path. The left wheels sank into the soft left shoulder. The car seemed to pull toward the left. If it kept going that way, it might cross the island and enter the lane carrying cars coming from the other direction.

Robert held on to the steering wheel. Then the left front wheel struck a rock, and the tire blew out. The car turned sideways. It was then that his mother began to scream.

As the car turned, it skidded part way out into the oncoming lanes. Robert Proctor fought the steering wheel to right the car. But the drag of the blown tire was too much. His mother's scream rang steadily in his ears. As he strained at the wheel, he wondered how a scream could go on so long.

An oncoming car struck his car from the side, and spun him farther into the left-hand lanes.

He was thrown into his mother's lap. She was thrown against the right door. It was locked and it held. With his left hand he grabbed the steering wheel. He pulled himself up. He turned the wheel to try to stop the spin so he could get his car out of traffic. His mother could not right herself. She lay against the door, her cry rising and falling with the spin of the car.

The car began to slow down. In one of the spins, he twisted the wheel straight and headed down the left-hand lane. Before he could turn off the pike to safety, a car loomed ahead of him.

The man at the wheel of that other car seemed unable to move. His eyes were wide and filled with fear. Beside him sat a girl with her head against the back of the seat. Soft curls framed her lovely face. She was asleep.

It was not the fear in the man's face that reached Robert Proctor. It was the trust in the face of the sleeping girl. In a flash the two cars sped closer to each other. Robert Proctor had no time to change the direction of his car.

The driver of the other car remained frozen at the wheel, Robert Proctor stared into the face of the sleeping girl. His mother's cry still sounded in his ears.

He heard no crash when the two cars met head on at high speed. He only felt something push into his stomach. Then the world went gray. Just before darkness came, he heard the scream stop. He knew then that he had been hearing one single scream. It had only seemed to drag on and on.

Robert Proctor seemed to be at the bottom of a deep black well. There was a spot of faint light in the far distance. He could hear the rumble of a voice. He tried to pull himself toward the light and the sound. But the effort was too great. He lay still and gathered his strength to try again. The light grew brighter and the voice louder. When he tried again, he seemed to draw closer to the light and sound. He opened his eyes and looked at the man sitting in front of him.

"You all right, son?" asked the man. He wore a blue uniform. His round face was familiar.

Robert Proctor moved his head slowly. He discovered that he was lying back in a chair. He could move his arms and legs. He looked around the room. Then he remembered.

The man in the uniform saw the look in Robert's eyes. He said, "No harm done, son. You just took the last part of your driver's test."

Robert Proctor looked at the man. Though he saw the man clearly, he seemed to see the faint face of the sleeping girl in front of him.

The uniformed man went on talking. "We hypnotized you to make you think you were in an accident. We do it to everybody these days before they get their driver's license. Makes better drivers of them. Makes drivers more careful for the rest of their lives. Remember it now? Coming in here and all?"

Robert Proctor nodded, thinking of the sleeping girl. She never would have awakened. She would have gone from her light sleep to the dark sleep of death. Worst of all would have been his mother's death.

The uniformed man was still speaking. "So you think you're all set now. If you still want a driver's license, sign this application and we'll see."

Robert Proctor looked at the license application and signed it.

He looked up to find two men in long white coats. They were standing one on each side of him. Somehow the sight of them made him angry.

He started to speak but the uniformed man spoke first. "Sorry, son. You failed your license test. You're sick and need treatment."

The two men lifted Robert Proctor to his feet. He said, "Take your hands off me. What is this?"

The uniformed man said, "Nobody should want to drive a car after going through what you just went through. It should take months before you can even think of driving again. But you're ready to drive right now. Killing people doesn't seem to bother you. We can't let your kind run around loose any more. But don't you worry, son. They'll take good care of you. They'll fix you up." He nodded to the two men. They began to march Robert Proctor out.

At the door he spoke. His voice was so full of pleading the two men paused. "You can't really mean this," he said. "I must still be dreaming. This is all part of the test, isn't it?"

The uniformed man said, "No, son, but you can try again later." They dragged Robert out the door, knees stiff, feet dragging. As they pulled, his rubber heels slid along the two grooves worn in the floor.

The Rocket

Ray Bradbury

**"I'll teach you!" he shouted.
But his hand stayed.**

Many nights Fiorello Bodoni would awaken to hear the rockets sighing in the dark sky. He would tiptoe from bed, certain that his kind wife was dreaming, to let himself out into the night air. For a few moments he would be free of the smells of old food in the small house by the river. For a silent moment he would let his heart soar alone into space, following the rockets.

Now, this very night, he stood half naked in the darkness, watching the fire fountains murmuring in the air. The rockets on their long wild way to Mars and Saturn and Venus!

"Well, well, Bodoni."

Bodoni started.

On a milk crate, by the silent river, sat an old man who also watched the rockets through the midnight hush.

"Oh, it's you, Bramante!"

"Do you come out every night, Bodoni?"

"Only for the air."

"So? I prefer the rockets myself," said old Bramante. "I was a boy when they started. Eighty years ago, and I've never been on one yet."

"I will ride up in one some day," said Bodoni.

"Fool!" cried Bramante. "You'll never go. This is a rich man's world." He shook his gray head, remembering. "When I was young

they wrote it in fiery letters: THE WORLD OF THE FUTURE!
Science, Comfort, and New Things for All! Ha! Eighty years. The
Future becomes Now! Do we fly rockets? No! We live in shacks like
our ancestors before us."

"Perhaps my sons —," said Bodoni.

"No, nor their sons!" the old man shouted. "It's the rich who have
dreams and rockets!"

Bodoni hesitated. "Old man, I've saved three thousand dollars. It
took me six years to save it. For my business, to invest in machinery.
But every night for a month now I've been awake. I hear the rockets. I
think. And tonight I've made up my mind. One of us will fly to Mars!"
His eyes were shining and dark.

"Idiot," snapped Bramante. "How will you choose? Who will go? If
you go, your wife will hate you, for you will be just a bit nearer God, in
space. When you tell your amazing trip to her, over the years, won't
bitterness gnaw at her?"

"No, no!"

"Yes! And your children? Will their lives be filled with the memory
of Papa, who flew to Mars while they stayed here? What a senseless
task you will set your boys. They will think of the rocket all their lives.
They will lie awake. They will be sick with wanting it. Just as you are
sick now. They will want to die if they cannot go. Don't set that goal, I
warn you. Let them be content with being poor. Turn their eyes down
to their hands and to your junk yard, not up to the stars."

"But —"

"Suppose your wife went. How would you feel, knowing she had
seen and you had not? She would become holy. You would think of
throwing her in the river. No, Bodoni, buy a new wrecking machine,
which you need, and pull your dreams apart with it, and smash them
to pieces."

The old man subsided, gazing at the river in which, drowned,
images of rockets burned down the sky.

"Good night," said Bodoni.

"Sleep well," said the other.

When the toast jumped from its silver box, Bodoni almost
screamed. The night had been sleepless. Among his nervous children,
beside his mountainous wife, Bodoni had twisted and stared at
nothing. Bramante was right. Better to invest the money. Why save it

when only one of the family could ride the rocket, while the others remained to melt in frustration?

"Fiorello, eat your toast," said his wife, Maria.

"My throat is shriveled," said Bodoni.

The children rushed in, the three boys fighting over a toy rocket, the two girls carrying dolls which duplicated the inhabitants of Mars, Venus, and Neptune, green mannequins with three yellow eyes and twelve fingers.

"I saw the Venus rocket!" cried Paolo.

"It took off, *whoosh!*" hissed Antonello.

"Children!" shouted Bodoni, hands to his ears.

They stared at him. He seldom shouted.

Bodoni arose. "Listen, all of you," he said. "I have enough money to take one of us on the Mars rocket."

Everyone yelled.

"You understand?" he asked. "Only one of us. Who?"

"Me, me, me!" cried the children.

"You," said Maria.

"You," said Bodoni to her.

They all fell silent.

"Think what you would see," said Bodoni's wife to him. But her eyes were strange. Her voice shook. "The meteors like fish. The universe. The Moon. Someone should go who could tell it well on returning. You have a way with words."

"Nonsense. So have you," he objected.

Everyone trembled.

"Here," said Bodoni unhappily. From a broom he broke straws of various lengths. "The short straw wins." He held out his tight fist. "Choose."

Solemnly each took a turn.

"Long straw."

"Long straw."

Another.

"Long straw."

The children finished. The room was quiet.

Two straws remained. Bodoni felt his heart ache in him. "Now," he whispered. "Maria."

She drew.

"The short straw," she said.

"Ah," sighed Lorenzo, half happy, half sad. "Mama goes to Mars."

Bodoni tried to smile. "Congratulations. I will buy your ticket today."

"Wait, Fiorello —"

"You can leave next week," he murmured.

She saw the sad eyes of her children upon her, with the smiles beneath their straight large noses. She returned the straw slowly to her husband. "I cannot go to Mars."

"But why not?"

"I will be busy with another child."

"What!"

She would not look at him. "It wouldn't do for me to travel in my condition."

He took her elbow. "Is this the truth?"

"Draw again. Start over."

"Why didn't you tell me before?" he said incredulously.

"I didn't remember."

"Maria, Maria," he whispered, patting her face. He turned to the children. "Draw again."

Paolo immediately drew the short straw.

"I go to Mars!" he danced wildly. "Thank you, Father!"

The other children edged away. "That's swell, Paolo."

Paolo stopped smiling to examine his parents and his brothers and sisters. "I can go, can't I?" he asked uncertainly.

"Yes."

"And you'll like me when I come back?"

"Of course."

Paolo studied the precious broomstraw on his trembling hand and shook his head. He threw it away. "I forgot. School starts. I can't go. Draw again."

But none would draw. A full sadness lay on them.

"None of us will go," said Lorenzo.

"That's best," said Maria.

"Bramante was right," said Bodoni.

With his breakfast curdled within him, Fiorello Bodoni worked in his junk yard, ripping metal, melting it, pouring out usable ingots. His equipment flaked apart; competition had kept him on the insane edge of poverty for twenty years. It was a very bad morning.

In the afternoon a man entered the junk yard and called up to Bodoni on his wrecking machine. "Hey, Bodoni. I got some metal for you!"

"What is it, Mr. Mathews?" asked Bodoni, listlessly.

"A rocket ship. What's wrong? Don't you want it?"

"Yes, yes!" He seized the man's arm and stopped, bewildered.

"Of course," said Mathews, "it's only a mockup. You know. When they plan a rocket they build a full-scale model first, of aluminum. You might make a small profit boiling her down. Let you have her for two thousand —"

Bodoni dropped his hand. "I haven't the money."

"Sorry. Thought I'd help you. Last time we talked you said how everyone outbid you on junk. Thought I'd slip this to you on the q.t. Well —"

"I need new equipment. I saved money for that."

"I understand."

"If I bought your rocket, I wouldn't even be able to melt it down. My aluminum furnace broke down last week —"

"Sure."

"I couldn't possibly use the rocket if I bought it from you."

"I know."

Bodoni blinked and shut his eyes. He opened them and looked at Mr. Mathews. "But I am a great fool. I will take my money from the bank and give it to you."

"But if you can't melt the rocket down —"

"Deliver it," said Bodoni.

"All right, if you say so. Tonight?"

"Tonight," said Bodoni, "would be fine. Yes, I would like to have a rocket ship tonight."

There was a moon. The rocket was white and big in the junk yard. It held the whiteness of the moon and the blueness of the stars. Bodoni looked at it and loved all of it. He wanted to pet it and lie against it, pressing it with his cheek, telling it all the secret wants of his heart.

He stared up at it, "You are all mine," he said. "Even if you never move or spit fire, and just sit there and rust for fifty years, you are mine."

The rocket smelled of time and distance. It was like walking into a clock. It was finished with Swiss delicacy. One might wear it on one's watch fob. "I might even sleep here tonight," Bodoni whispered excitedly.

He sat in the pilot's seat.

He touched a lever.

He hummed in his shut mouth, his eyes closed.

The humming grew louder, louder, higher, higher, wilder, stranger, more exhilarating, trembling in him and leaning him forward and pulling him and the ship in a roaring silence and in a kind of metal screaming, while his fists flew over the controls, and his shut eyes quivered, and the sound grew and grew until it was a fire, a strength, a lifting and a pushing of power that threatened to tear him in half. He gasped. He hummed again and again, and did not stop, for it would not be stopped, it could only go on, his eyes tighter, his heart furious. "Taking off!" he screamed. *The jolting concussion! The thunder!* "The Moon!" he cried, eyes blind, tight. "The meteors!" *The silent rush in volcanic light.* "Mars. Oh, God, Mars! Mars!"

He fell back, exhausted and panting. His shaking hands came loose of the controls and his head tilted back wildly. He sat for a long time, breathing out and in, his heart slowing.

Slowly, slowly, he opened his eyes.

The junk yard was still there.

He sat motionless. He looked at the heaped piles of metal for a minute, his eyes never leaving them. Then, leaping up, he kicked the levers. "Take off, damn you!"

The ship was silent.

"I'll show you!" he cried.

Out in the night air, stumbling, he started the fierce motor of his terrible wrecking machine and advanced upon the rocket. He maneuvered the massive weights into the moonlit sky. He readied his trembling hands to plunge the weights, to smash, to rip apart this insolently false dream, this silly thing for which he had paid his money, which would not move, which would not do his bidding. "I'll teach you!" he shouted.

But his hand stayed.

The silver rocket lay in the light of the moon. And beyond the rocket stood the yellow lights of his home, a block away, burning warmly. He heard the family radio playing some distant music. He sat for half an hour considering the rocket and the house lights, and his

eyes narrowed and grew wide. He stepped down from the wrecking machine and began to walk, and as he walked he began to laugh, and when he reached the back door of his house he took a deep breath and called, "Maria, Maria, start packing. We're going to Mars!"

"Oh!"

"Ah!"

"I can't *believe* it!"

"You will, you will."

The children balanced in the windy yard, under the glowing rocket, not touching it yet. They started to cry.

Maria looked at her husband. "What have you done?" she said. "Taken our money for this? It will never fly."

"It will fly," he said looking at it.

"Rocket ships cost millions. Have you millions?"

"It will fly," he repeated steadily. "Now, go to the house, all of you. I have phone calls to make, work to do. Tomorrow we leave. Tell no one, understand? It is a secret."

The children edged off from the rocket, stumbling. He saw their small, feverish faces in the house windows, far away.

Maria had not moved. "You have ruined us," she said. "Our money used for this — this thing. When it should have been spent on equipment."

"You will see," he said.

Without a word she turned away.

"God help me," he whispered, and started to work.

Through the midnight hours trucks arrived, packages were delivered, and Bodoni, smiling, exhausted his bank account. With blowtorch and metal stripping he assaulted the rocket, added, took away, worked fiery magics and secret insults upon it. He bolted nine ancient automobile motors into the rocket's empty engine room. Then he welded the engine room shut, so none could see his hidden labor.

At dawn he entered the kitchen. "Maria," he said, "I'm ready for breakfast."

She would not speak to him.

At sunset he called to the children. "We're ready! Come out!" The house was silent.

"I've locked them in the closet," said Maria.

"What do you mean?" he demanded.

"You'll be killed in that rocket," she said. "What kind of rocket can you buy for two thousand dollars? A bad one!"

"Listen to me, Maria."

"It will blow up. Anyway, you are no pilot."

"Nevertheless, I can fly *this* ship. I have fixed it."

"You have gone mad," she said.

"Where is the key to the closet?"

"I have it here."

He put out his hand. "Give it to me."

She handed it to him. "You will kill them."

"No, no."

"Yes, you will. I *feel* it."

He stood before her. "You won't come along?"

"I'll stay here," she said.

"You will understand, you will see then," he said, and smiled. He unlocked the closet. "Come children. Follow your father."

"Good-by, good-by, Mama!"

She stayed in the kitchen window, looking out at them, very straight and silent.

At the door of the rocket the father said, "Children, we will be gone a week. You must come back to school, and I to my business." He took each of their hands in turn. "Listen. This rocket is very old and will fly only *one* more journey. It will not fly again. This will be the one trip of your life. Keep your eyes wide."

"Yes, Papa."

"Listen, keep your ears clean. Smell the smells of a rocket. *Feel. Remember.* So when you return you will talk of it all the rest of your lives."

"Yes, Papa."

The ship was quiet as a stopped clock. The airlock hissed shut behind them. He strapped them all, like tiny mummies, into rubber hammocks. "Ready?" he called.

"Ready!" all replied.

"Take-off!" He jerked ten switches. The rocket thundered and leaped. The children danced in their hammocks, screaming.

"Here comes the Moon!"

The moon dreamed by. Meteors broke into fireworks. Time flowed away in a serpentine of gas. The children shouted. Released from their hammocks, hours later, they peered from the ports. "There's Earth!" "There's Mars!"

The rocket dropped pink petals of fire while the hour dials spun; the children's eyes dropped shut. At last they hung like drunken moths in their cocoon hammocks.

"Good," whispered Bodoni, alone.

He tiptoed from the control room to stand for a long moment fearful, at the airlock door.

He pressed a button. The airlock door swung wide. He stepped out. Into space? Into inky tides of meteor and gaseous torch? Into swift mileages and infinite dimensions?

No. Bodoni smiled.

All about the quivering rocket lay the junk yard.

Rusting, unchanged, there stood the padlocked junk yard gate, the little silent house by the river, the kitchen window lighted, and the river going down to the same sea. And in the center of the junk yard, manufacturing a magic dream, lay the quivering, purring rocket. Shaking and roaring, bouncing the netted children like flies in a web.

Maria stood in the kitchen window.

He waved to her and smiled.

He could not see if she waved or not. A small wave, perhaps. A small smile.

The sun was rising.

Bodoni withdrew hastily into the rocket. Silence. All still slept. He breathed easily. Tying himself into a hammock, he closed his eyes. To himself he prayed, Oh, let nothing happen to the illusion in the next six days. Let all of space come and go, and red Mars come up under our ship, and the moons of Mars, and let there be no flaws in the color film. Let there be three dimensions; let nothing go wrong with the hidden mirrors and screens that mold the fine illusion. Let time pass without crisis.

He awoke.

Red Mars floated near the rocket.

"Papa!" The children thrashed to be free.

Bodoni looked and saw red Mars and it was good and there was no flaw in it and he was very happy.

At sunset on the seventh day the rocket stopped shuddering.

"We are home," said Bodoni.

They walked across the junk yard from the open door of the rocket, their blood singing, their faces glowing.

"I have ham and eggs for all of you," said Maria, at the kitchen door.

"Mama, Mama, you should have come, to see it, to see Mars, Mama, and meteors, and everything!"

"Yes," she said.

At bedtime the children gathered before Bodoni. "We want to thank you, Papa."

"It was nothing."

"We will remember it for always, Papa. We will never forget."

Very late in the night Bodoni opened his eyes. He sensed that his wife was lying beside him, watching him. She did not move for a very long time and then suddenly she kissed his cheeks and his forehead. "What's this?" he cried.

"You're the best father in the world," she whispered.

"Why?"

"Now I see," she said. "I understand."

She lay back and closed her eyes, holding his hand. "Is it a very lovely journey?" she asked.

"Yes," he said.

"Perhaps," she said, "perhaps, some night you might take me on just a little trip, do you think?"

"Just a little one, perhaps," he said.

"Thank you," she said. "Good night."

"Good night," said Fiorello Bodoni.

Mariana

Fritz Leiber

**She was alone on an infinite flat rock plain
under the cloudless star-specked sky.**

Mariana had been living in the big villa and hating the tall pine
trees around it for what seemed like an eternity when she found the
secret panel in the master control panel of the house.

The secret panel was simply a narrow blank of aluminum — she'd
thought of it as room for more switches if they ever needed any, perish
the thought! — between the air-conditioning controls and the gravity
controls. Above the switches for the three-dimensional TV but below
those for the robot butler and maids.

Jonathan had told her not to fool with the master control panel
while he was in the city, so when the secret panel came loose under her
aimlessly questing fingers and fell to the solid rock floor of the patio
with a musical *twing* her first reaction was fear.

Then she saw it was only a small blank oblong of sheet aluminum
that had fallen and that in the space it had covered was a column of six
little switches. Only the top one was identified. Tiny glowing letters
beside it spelled TREES and it was on.

When Jonathan got home from the city that evening she gathered
her courage and told him about it. He was neither particularly angry
nor impressed.

"Of course there's a switch for the trees," he informed her deflat-
ingly, motioning the robut butler to cut his steak. "Didn't you know
they were radio trees? I didn't want to wait twenty-five years for them
and they couldn't grow in this rock anyway. A station in the city
broadcasts a master pine tree and sets like ours pick it up and project it
around homes. It's vulgar but convenient."

After a bit she asked timidly, "Jonathan, are the radio pine trees ghostly as you drive through them?"

"Of course not! They're solid as this house and the rock under it — to the eye and to the touch too. A person could even climb them. If you ever stirred outside you'd know these things. The city station transmits pulses of alternating matter at sixty cycles a second."

She ventured one more question: "Why did they have the tree switch covered up?"

"So you wouldn't monkey with it — same as the fine controls on the TV. And so you wouldn't get ideas and start changing the trees. It would unsettle *me*, let me tell you, to come home to oaks one day and birches the next. I like consistency and I like pines." He looked at them out of the dining-room picture window and grunted with satisfaction.

She had been meaning to tell him about hating the pines, but that discouraged her and she dropped the topic.

About noon the next day, however, she went to the secret panel and switched off the pine trees and quickly turned around to watch them.

At first nothing happened and she was beginning to think that Jonathan was wrong again, as he so often was though would never admit, but then they began to waver and specks of pale green light churned across them and then they faded and were gone, leaving behind only an intolerably bright single point of light — just as when the TV is switched off. The star hovered motionless for what seemed a long time, then backed away and faced off toward the horizon.

Now that the pine trees were out of the way Mariana could see the real landscape. It was flat gray rock, endless miles of it, exactly the same as the rock on which the house was set and which formed the floor of the patio. It was the same in every direction. One black two-lane road drove straight across it — nothing more.

She disliked the view almost at once — it was dreadfully lonely and depressing. She switched the gravity to moon-normal and danced about dreamily, floating over the middle-of-the-room bookshelves and the grand piano and even having the robot maids dance with her, but it did not cheer her. About two o'clock she went to switch on the pine trees again, as she had intended to do in any case before Jonathan came home and was furious.

However, she found there had been changes in the column of six little switches. The TREES switch no longer had its glowing name. She remembered that it had been the top one, but the top one would not turn on again. She tried to force it from "off" to "on" but it would not move.

All of the rest of the afternoon she sat on the steps outside the front door watching the black two-lane road. Never a car or a person came into view until Jonathan's tan roadster appeared, seeming at first to hang motionless in the distance and then to move only like a microscopic snail although she knew he always drove at top speed — it was one of the reasons she would never get in the car with him.

Jonathan was not as furious as she had feared. "Your own fault for meddling with it," he said curtly. "Now we'll have to get somebody out here. I hate to eat supper looking at nothing but those rocks! Bad enough driving through them twice a day."

She asked him haltingly about the barrenness of the landscape and the absence of neighbors.

"Well, you wanted to live *way out*," he told her. "You wouldn't ever have known about it if you hadn't turned off the trees."

"There's one other thing I've got to bother you with, Jonathan," she said. "Now the second switch — the one next below — has got a name that glows. It just says HOUSE. It's turned on — I haven't touched it! Do you suppose . . ."

"I want to look at this," he said, bounding up from the couch and slamming his martini-on-the-rocks tumbler down on the tray of the robot maid so that she rattled. "I bought this house as solid, but there are swindles. Ordinarily I'd spot a broadcast style in a flash, but they just might have slipped me a job relayed from some other planet or solar system. Fine thing if me and fifty other multi-megabuck men were spotted around in identical houses, each thinking his was unique."

"But if the house is based on rock like it is . . ."

"That would just make it easier for them to pull the trick."

They reached the master control panel. "There it is," she said helpfully, jabbing out a finger . . . and hit the HOUSE switch.

For a moment nothing happened, then a white churning ran across the ceiling, the walls and furniture started to swell and bubble like cold lava, and then they were alone on a rock table big as three tennis courts. Even the master control panel was gone. The only thing that was left was a slender rod coming out of the gray stone at their feet and bearing at the top, like some mechanistic fruit, a small block with the six switches — that and an intolerably bright star hanging in the air where the master bedroom had been.

Mariana pushed frantically at the HOUSE switch, but it was unlabeled now and locked in the "off" position, although she threw her weight at it stiff-armed.

The upstairs star sped off like an incendiary bullet, but its last flashbulb glare showed her Jonathan's face set in lines of fury. He lifted his hands like talons.

"You little idiot!" he screamed, coming at her.

"No, Jonathan, no!" she wailed, backing off, but he kept coming.

She realized that the block of switches had broken off in her hands. The third switch had a glowing name now: JONATHAN. She flipped it.

As his fingers dug into her bare shoulders they seemed to turn to foam rubber, then to air. His face and gray flannel suit seethed iridescently, like a leprous ghost's, then melted and ran. His star, smaller than that of the house but much closer, seared her eyes. When she opened them again there was nothing at all left of the star or Jonathan but a dancing dark afterimage like a black tennis ball.

She was alone on an infinite flat rock plain under the cloudless, star-specked sky.

The fourth switch had its glowing name now: STARS.

It was almost dawn by her radium-dialed wristwatch and she was thoroughly chilled when she finally decided to switch off the stars. She did not want to do it—in their slow wheeling across the sky they were the last sign of orderly reality—but it seemed the only move she could make.

She wondered what the fifth switch would say, ROCKS. AIR. Or even . . .?

She switched off the stars.

The Milky Way, arching in all its unalterable glory, began to churn, its component stars darting about like midges. Soon only one remained, brighter even than Sirius or Venus — until it jerked back, fading, and darted to infinity.

The fifth switch said DOCTOR and it was not on but off.

An inexplicable terror welled up in Mariana. She did not want to touch the fifth switch. She set the block of switches down on the rock and backed away from it.

But she dared not go far in the starless dark. She huddled down and waited for dawn. From time to time she looked at her watch dial and at the night-light glow of the switchlabel a dozen yards away.

It seemed to be growing much colder.

She read her watch dial. It was two hours past sunrise. She remembered they had taught her in third grade that the sun was just one more star.

She went back and sat down beside the block of switches and picked it up with a shudder and flipped the fifth switch.

The rock grew soft and crisply fragrant under her and lapped up over her legs and then slowly turned white.

She was sitting in a hospital bed in a small blue room with a white pinstripe.

A sweet, mechanical voice came out of the wall, saying, "You have interrupted the wish-fulfillment therapy by your own decision. If you now recognize your sick depression and are willing to accept help, the doctor will come to you. If not, you are at liberty to return to the wish-fulfillment therapy and pursue it to its ultimate conclusion."

Mariana looked down. She still had the block of switches in her hands and the fifth switch still read DOCTOR.

The wall said, "I assume from your silence that you will accept treatment. The doctor will be with you immediately."

The inexplicable terror returned to Mariana with compulsive intensity.

She switched off the doctor.

She was back in the starless dark. The rocks had grown very much colder. She could feel icy feathers falling on her face — snow.

She lifted the block of switches and saw, to her unutterable relief, that the sixth and last switch now read, in tiny glowing letters: MARIANA.

Annabelle, I Love You

Mildred Clingerman

I think I have died and gone to hell.
There wasn't anybody at Annabelle's
house. There *hadn't been* anybody at
Annabelle's house!

Jan. 12. Keeping a journal may well be a revolting habit, but people have been doing it for centuries. I wonder if, like me, they began because they were lonely and sick and bitter? No. Some of them began out of joy. I wonder what joy looks like. That was one of the things I thought about in the hospital, with my eyes and ears closed against all the gabby, false-bright voices of the women in the room with me. Behind my closed eyelids I guessed that joy was an exploding star, like the sun: dangerous to one's health if exposed too long to its rays.

I've just come out of the hospital again. This was my second bout with pneumonia since November. I'm still sick, but they needed my bed for somebody sicker. I've had to take a long leave of absence from my job. My house has that smeared, smudged look houses get when they're left cold and empty. I wish Danny hadn't forced it on me in the divorce settlement. He was feeling guilty, of course, and I was too diminished to argue.

Jan. 13. Disorder is everywhere — in me, in this house, in my checkbook, in the weather, in the whole street. The garbage collectors have just come and gone, strewing bits of garbage behind them like kings flinging largess to the populace. In my saggy blue bathrobe with my uncombed hair I stand for a few minutes at the window staring out, thinking about this street, and I see it winding its way across the nation. It's a bedroom street and a transition street, I decide. People move from here either up or down the economic scale and rehouse themselves accordingly. Nobody stays very long. Somebody, even now, is taking down the FOR SALE signs on the house next door. I never met the last set of owners. Our paths never crossed. Danny and I both worked, as do most of our neighbors. I doubt if anybody on the street knows or cares that Danny moved out over a year ago.

Weakness forces me back to the bed I've made on the sofa. I can't rest in my lonely king-size bed. I listen to the wind moaning around the corners of the house, and I can imagine it peering down my chimney at the old dead ashes. There's plenty of wood in the woodbox and more on the woodpile. Perhaps tonight I'll build a fire. Now I have something warming to think about. All day I can lie here and plan the fire I'll build. I'll think out every move. First, the wadded newspaper. I wonder if the wind has blown away all the yellowing newspapers in the entry? First, I'll open the front door and bring in the newspapers, all of them. If not today, then tomorrow, for sure. And I'll heat up a can of soup. Tomorrow. I really will.

Jan. 15. Yesterday was nothing. It must have been nothing, because I remember nothing. This morning, though, began when I found myself standing thirsty at the kitchen sink. I drank some water and took two pills the doctor made me promise I'd take. Till now I'd forgotten to take them. I thought about coffee. The kitchen window gives me a good view of the house next door. Somebody is moving in. The wind is still blowing, and a young woman in a fur coat stands outside near the moving van while the men unload furniture. On her head she is wearing a heavy red scarf which falls into beautiful ripples and folds as the wind plays with it. There is no chaos around her. The furniture being unloaded arranges itself in order and beauty. She directs the movers, and the pieces are carried inside in patterned sanity. Nothing blows away. Nothing is smashed. It is a ballet, and, wobbly-legged, I cling to the sink while I watch entranced. How queer that I'm back on the sofa scribbling in my security-blanket journal. Perhaps I dreamed the ballet. What happened to the coffee? Did I leave it in the kitchen? (If I was in the kitchen.) It's too far to go back now.

Jan. 16. (I think) The young woman's name is Annabelle. She has a husband who owns a plumbing supply shop, and they have two small children, both girls, who are staying with their grandmother till the moving-in chores are completed. They plan to live here forever. Once they've added a room onto it, the house next door is the house of their dreams. Their grandchildren will visit them there in the misty, dim future, she says. She rang my doorbell yesterday. I always used to believe that poem that says you will never know with a doorbell who will be ringing it. But I knew with this ringing exactly who it was. Such a beautifully precise ring—no sloppy punch-punching at the button. I thought about not answering. I couldn't find my old runover house slippers. They were lost under the blanket on the sofa. Never mind the house slippers. I was wearing my saggy blue robe, and there was enough furniture to hang onto almost all the way to the door. It took a while to unbolt the door. Sometimes when I first wake up I can't read the clock staring me right in the face, and I can't make mechanical things work —like bolted doors or automatic coffee makers.

Annabelle can make anything work. She led me back to the sofa, covered me and then worked the can opener and the coffee pot and set up a tray for me. She found my hairbrush and soap and water and towel and tidied me up while the soup heated. She was quiet and small and warm. She had come to use the telephone to order a telephone for herself. She was a good long while, but I was too dazed with hot food and coffee and tidiness to pay any attention to the calls she made.

She came away from the phone with the name of one of her mother's distant cousins who would love to come and take care of me and my house. Who else in this city but Annabelle would have a widowed cousin just standing by eager to serve a next-door stranger?

Jan. 18. H. C. (Handy Cousin) is now installed in the guest room. She is an older version of Annabelle-ness. Though I still cling to the sofa, the house and I are tidied beyond belief. I am exhausted. I have been forced into hot, scented baths, pristine nightgowns and my best pink robe. My old slippers no longer hide under the blanket on the sofa. No. My best take-to-the-hospital ones stand neatly side by side on the vacuumed rug. H.C.'s real name is Rosalie, but I persist in calling her H.C. for short. She just laughs. She looks like a tubby little gray pony with neat hooves that stamp, stamp all around the house demolishing disorder. She is an automatic producer of hot heartening food, click, click, every two hours.

When Annabelle can break away from her joyous order next door, she comes to survey mine with twinkling satisfaction. She brings me grapes and tangerines and small, delightful books to browse through.

The books are not too heavy to hold when one is lying down. They even stay open at the page one is reading when laid aside for a while. Annabelle flings all this bounty down on the coffee table, and it arranges itself into a still-life painting. Oak logs mutter steadily in the fireplace. The polished brass fender gleams. Warmth envelops me. I am cozy.

I say, "Annabelle, I hate you. You're too perfect. Everything you do is perfect," and she laughs. She doesn't protest that she has done "nothing . . . nothing." She simply states, "You'd do the same for any neighbor."

I don't know that I would, actually. And certainly I couldn't have done any of it half so gracefully.

Jan. 20. H.C. was called away today, and I am now on my own. I wrote out a generous check for her, but she said it was too much and she would send me a proper bill later. I hate tearing up checks and writing "void" in my check register. It feels too much like a comment on my life. H.C. hurried away to Anabelle's house, where, apparently, she was to be picked up and passed on by Annabelle's husband to some worthier, more challenging case than mine. For I am getting well, and H.C. has no use for people who are getting well and whose houses are in order.

In the afternoon I heard a creaking of wheels and a low murmur of voices. I looked out the front window and saw Annabelle pushing a very old-fashioned baby buggy up the front walk. She was accompanied by a little girl who was carrying a jam jar filled with narcissus. I watched Annabelle park the buggy in the thin sunshine, set the brake carefully and tilt the adjustable top to shade the baby's face. She and the little girl stood smiling and gazing into the buggy for a moment, before they turned away to ring my doorbell.

When I opened the door Annabelle's daughter presented me with the flowers shyly, but in the little white triangle of her face her mouth was half-widened with the fun of a visit and a gift to a new, weird neighbor. But she wouldn't come in. She must stay outside, she said, to keep watch over her baby sister. I guessed that Annabelle was reluctant to bring either of her treasures inside where some stubborn germ might be lurking. But nothing today could dampen my spirits. Annabelle and I stood at the window talking. No. That's not true. Annabelle listened, her eyes soft and loving, while I waxed lyrical —

raving about the beauty of the day, of her children adorning my front walk, deserving, I said, a master painter's eye and hand. I was seeing great paintings everywhere: the street outside with all the garbage picked up by Annabelle's husband, curving its way between the houses, and hinting, after all, at hope and work and achievement; the bare, beige-colored chinaberry tree looking against the blue sky like a lacquered Chinese screen. I wait for Annabelle's comment on these wonders.

Annabelle answers simply that people recovering from an illness see the world with new, refreshed eyes. Moreover, she suggests, beauty is in the eye of the beholder and why don't I study painting, myself? She has this address of a man two streets over who is a real artist, who has paintings hanging all over the world and who will think about giving me lessons, if he can stand me. Annabelle doesn't really say that last bit, but hints delicately that the artist is rather difficult. She finds a pencil and scribbles the address on the back of an old envelope. When she hands it to me, some small explosion takes place behind my eyes. I think it might be joy.

Jan. 22. Yesterday I was strong enough to dress and drive down to the shopping center. Besides loading up with all sorts of supplies for the pantry and the house, I gave myself the pleasure of gathering gifts and goodies for Annabelle's children. By the time I got all the food refrigerated and stored away, I collapsed, of course, on my sofa and slept there till bedtime. But this afternoon I mean to walk over to Annabelle's house and revel in all its glories. I want to see Annabelle rocking the baby. I want to hear little triangle face laugh at the funny doll I've brought her. I want to warm myself at their fire.

Later: I think I have died and gone to hell. There wasn't anybody at Annabelle's house. There hadn't been anybody at Annabelle's house. I stood in the unswept entry and rang and rang the bell. Tattered FOR SALE signs were driven into the dead lawn on each side of the walk. I stumbled around to the back of the house and looked into the uncurtained kitchen window. Nobody had cooked a meal in that kitchen for months. I don't remember how I got myself home again. But here I am, shaking and scribbling, trying to fumble my way up and out of the windy, terrifying dark. I have turned all the lights on and the furnace up, but nothing warms my freezing grief.

Again later: Who cleaned the house? For it is clean — reasonably clean. I look around for the delightful, small books. There are only my books. The fruit in the bowl is the fruit I bought yesterday. But there sits the jam jar with the dying narcissus! The whole room is scented with them. And there on my old slant-top desk is the envelope with the scribbled address . . . it is not my handwriting, surely?

Some nagging memory makes me kneel on the floor to open the heavy bottom drawer of the desk. It is filled with old family albums and mementos left to me when my grandmother died. I shall spend the rest of this night going through them.

Jan. 23. By ten o'clock this morning I was ringing the doorbell at the address written on the envelope. A man's voice roared at me for goodness sake to cease that incessant ringing and come on in. I did. He was standing in the middle of the living room, bracing himself against a chair and waving a coffee pot at me. One leg was in a "walking" cast, and his right arm was in a sling.

"Can you make coffee?" he asked. I said I could most times.

"Then do it," he said. He waved me towards the kitchen and stumped after me.

I cooked breakfast for both of us. Together we built up the fire in the fireplace and settled on the lumpy sofa to finish up the coffee. I asked him to take me as a student. By noon he had agreed to do so.

"You'll probably make a lousy painter," he said. "But you make good coffee."

He told me he had broken his leg and sprained his wrist by falling off a rickety chair while he was trying to replace burnt-out light bulbs in the studio, but that his injuries wouldn't affect either his teaching or his painting, since he was left-handed, anyway.

After touring the studio and surviving the heart and belly blows of his magnificent paintings, I felt strong enough to cook lunch for both of us. By three o'clock in the afternoon I was in possession of all the important bits of his life story. By suppertime he knew all about mine, including yesterday's hideous shock, and how I had found healing in the family photograph albums. I told him that my parents and small sister had died in an automobile accident when I was a baby and that I had been brought up by my grandmother.

"And your mother's name was . . .?" he asked gently.

"Annabelle, of course. I was the baby in the old-fashioned pram."

"And you believe your young mother came back to help you?"

"It warms me to think so. It takes the tight bands off my heart. It eases me," I said.

"I can understand and maybe, even, believe all of it—the way you do—except the part about giving you my address," he said. "How and why, would your ghost-mother have come by that?"

"I don't know." I shook my head. "I don't understand that part, either."

He was silent for a long time and then emitted a short bark of laughter. "This H.C. who trot-trotted around the house . . . you didn't tell me what her real name was."

"Rosalie."

"My God, girl! That's it." He hugged me with his sound left arm. "Mothers are fantastic. Even long-dead ones. They always think they know what's best for their children — even aging old crocks like me. Rosalie was my mother's name!" He was grinning with delight. "You described her perfectly."

"You mean she passed your name on to Annabelle so I would come and help you? I don't believe it . . . I don't believe you. You're making the whole thing up. I'll bet your mother's name was something entirely different — like Agnes, or Sadie."

"Believe, girl, believe! This relationship was made in heaven." He kissed me for quite a long time.

I began to believe.

One Ordinary Day, With Peanuts

Shirley Jackson

The man wanting a dime took
the peanut because Mr. Johnson
had wrapped a dollar bill
around it.

Mr. John Philip Johnson shut his front door behind him and came down his front steps into the bright morning with a feeling that all was well with the world on this best of all days, and wasn't the sun warm and good, and didn't his shoes feel comfortable after the resoling, and he knew that he had undoubtedly chosen the precise very tie which belonged with the day and the sun and his comfortable feet, and, after all, wasn't the world just a wonderful place? In spite of the fact that he was a small man, and the tie was perhaps a shade vivid, Mr. Johnson irradiated this feeling of well-being as he came down the steps and onto the dirty sidewalk, and he smiled at people who passed him, and some of them even smiled back. He stopped at the newsstand on the corner and bought his paper, saying "Good morning" with real conviction to the man who sold him the paper and the two or three other people who were lucky enough to be buying papers with candy and peanuts, and then he set out to get himself uptown. He stopped in a flower shop and bought a carnation for his buttonhole, and stopped almost immediately afterward to give the carnation to a small child in a carriage, who looked at him and then smiled, and Mr. Johnson smiled, and the child's mother looked at Mr. Johnson for a minute and then smiled too.

When he had gone several blocks uptown, Mr. Johnson cut across the avenue and went along a side street, chosen at random; he did not follow the same route every morning, but preferred to pursue his eventful way in wide detours more like a puppy than a man intent upon business. It happened this morning that halfway down the block a moving van was parked, and the furniture from an upstairs apartment stood half on the sidewalk, half on the steps, while an amused group of people loitered, examining the scratches on the tables and the worn spots on the chairs, and a harassed woman, trying to watch a young child and the movers and the furniture all at the same time, gave the clear impression of endeavoring to shelter her private life from the people staring at her belongings. Mr. Johnson stopped, and for a moment joined the crowd, and then he came forward and, touching his hat civilly, said, "Perhaps I can keep an eye on your little boy for you?"

The woman turned and glared at him distrustfully, and Mr. Johnson added hastily, "We'll sit right here on the steps." He beckoned to the little boy, who hesitated and then responded agreeably to Mr. Johnson's genial smile. Mr. Johnson brought out a handful of peanuts from his pocket and sat on the steps with the boy, who at first refused the peanuts on the grounds that his mother did not allow him to accept food from strangers; Mr. Johnson said that probably his mother had not intended peanuts to be included, since elephants at the circus ate them, and the boy considered, and then agreed solemnly. They sat on the steps cracking peanuts in a comradely fashion, and Mr. Johnson said, "So you're moving?"

"Yep," said the boy.

"Where you going?"

"Nice place. Plenty of snow there. Maple sugar, too; you like maple sugar?"

"Sure."

"Plenty of maple sugar in Vermont. You going to live on a farm?"

"Going to live with Grandpa."

"Grandpa like peanuts?"

"Sure."

"Ought to take him some," said Mr. Johnson, reaching into his pocket. "Just you and Mommy going?"

"Yep."

"Tell you what," Mr. Johnson said. "You take some peanuts to eat on the train."

The boy's mother, after glancing at them frequently, had seemingly decided that Mr. Johnson was trustworthy, because she had devoted herself wholeheartedly to seeing that the movers did not — what movers rarely do, but everybody believes they will—crack a leg from a table, or set a kitchen chair down on a lamp. Most of the furniture was loaded by now, and she was deep in that nervous stage when she knew there was something she had forgotten to pack — hidden away in the back of a closet somewhere, or left at a neighbor's and forgotten, or on the clothesline—and was trying to remember under stress what it was.

"This all, lady?" the chief mover said, completing her dismay.

Uncertainly, she nodded.

"Want to go on the truck with the furniture, sonny?" the mover asked the boy, and laughed. The boy laughed too and said to Mr. Johnson, "I guess I'll have a good time in Vermont."

"Fine time," said Mr. Johnson, and stood up. "Have one more peanut before you go," he said to the boy.

The boy's mother said to Mr. Johnson, "Thank you so much; it was a great help to me."

"Nothing at all," said Mr. Johnson gallantly. "Where in Vermont are you going?"

The mother looked at the little boy accusingly, as though he had given away a secret of some importance, and said unwillingly, "Greenwich".

"Lovely town," said Mr. Johnson. He took out a card, and wrote a name on the back. "Very good friend of mine lives in Greenwich," he said. "Call on him for anything you need. His wife makes the best doughnuts in town," he added soberly to the little boy.

"Swell," said the little boy.

"Goodbye," said Mr. Johnson.

He went on, stepping happily with his new-shod feet, feeling the warm sun on his back and on the top of his head. Halfway down the block he met a stray dog and fed him a peanut.

At the corner, where another wide avenue faced him, Mr. Johnson decided to go on uptown again. Moving with comparative laziness, he was passed on either side by people hurrying and frowning, and people brushed past him going the other way, clattering along to get somewhere quickly. Mr. Johnson stopped on every corner and waited patiently for the light to change, and he stepped out of the way of anyone who seemed to be in any particular hurry, but one young lady came too fast for him, and crashed wildly into him when he stooped to pat a kitten which had run out onto the sidewalk from an apartment house and was now unable to get back through the rushing feet.

"Excuse me," said the young lady, trying frantically to pick up Mr. Johnson and hurry on at the same time, "terribly sorry."

The kitten, regardless now of danger, raced back to its home. "Perfectly all right," said Mr. Johnson, adjusting himself carefully. "You seem to be in a hurry."

"Of course I'm in a hurry," said the young lady. "I'm late."

She was extremely cross and the frown between her eyes seemed well on its way to becoming permanent. She had obviously awakened late, because she had not spent any extra time in making herself look pretty, and her dress was plain, and her lipstick was noticeably crooked. She tried to brush past Mr. Johnson, but, risking her suspicious displeasure, he took her arm and said, "Please wait."

"Look," she said ominously, "I ran into you and your lawyer can see my lawyer and I will gladly pay all damages and all inconveniences suffered therefrom, but please this minute let me go because I am late."

"Late for what?" said Mr. Johnson; he tried his winning smile on her but it did no more than keep her, he suspected, from knocking him down again.

"Late for work," she said between her teeth. "Late for my employment. I have a job and if I am late I lose exactly so much an hour and I cannot really afford what your pleasant conversation is costing me, be it ever so pleasant."

"I'll pay for it," said Mr. Johnson. Now these were magic words, not necessarily because they were true, or because she seriously expected Mr. Johnson to pay for anything, but because Mr. Johnson's flat statement, obviously innocent of irony, could not be, coming from

Mr. Johnson, anything but the statement of a responsible and truthful and respectable man.

"What do you mean?" she asked.

"I said that since I am obviously responsible for your being late I shall certainly pay for it "

"Don't be silly," she said, and for the first time the frown disappeared. "I wouldn't expect you to pay for anything—a few minutes ago I was offering to pay you. Anyway," she added, almost smiling, "it was my fault."

"What happens if you don't go to work?"

She stared. "I don't get paid."

"Precisely," said Mr. Johnson.

"What do you mean, precisely? If I don't show up at the office exactly twenty minutes ago I lose a dollar and twenty cents an hour, or two cents a minute or . . ." She thought. ". . . Almost a dime for the time I've spent talking to you."

Mr. Johnson laughed, and finally she laughed, too. "You're late already," he pointed out. "Will you give me another four cents' worth?"

"I don't understand why."

"You'll see," Mr. Johnson promised. He led her over to the side of the walk, next to the buildings, and said, "Stand here," and went out into the rush of people going both ways. Selecting and considering, as one who must make a choice involving perhaps whole years of lives, he estimated the people going by. Once he almost moved, and then at the last minute thought better of it and drew back. Finally, from half a block away, he saw what he wanted, and moved out into the center of the traffic to intercept a young man, who was hurrying, and dressed as though he had awakened late, and frowning.

"Oof," said the young man, because Mr. Johnson had thought of no better way to intercept anyone than the one the young woman had unwittingly used upon him. "Where do you think you're going?" the young man demanded from the sidewalk.

"I want to speak to you," said Mr. Johnson ominously.

The young man got up nervously, dusting himself and eyeing Mr. Johnson. "What for?" he said. "What'd I do?"

"That's what bothers me most about people nowadays," Mr. Johnson complained broadly to the people passing. "No matter whether they've done anything or not, they always figure someone's after them. About what you're going to do," he told the young man.

"Listen," said the young man, trying to brush past him. "I'm late, and I don't have any time to listen. Here's a dime, now get going."

"Thank you," said Mr. Johnson, pocketing the dime. "Look," he said, "what happens if you stop running?"

"I'm late," said the young man, still trying to get past Mr. Johnson, who was unexpectedly clinging.

"How much you make an hour?" Mr. Johnson demanded.

"A communist, are you?" said the young man. "Now will you please let me —"

"No," said Mr. Johnson insistently, "how much?"

"Dollar fifty," said the young man. "And now will you —"

"You like adventure?"

The young man stared, and staring, found himself caught and held by Mr. Johnson's genial smile; he almost smiled back and then repressed it and made an effort to tear away. "I got to hurry," he said.

"Mystery? Like surprises? Unusual and exciting events?"

"You selling something?"

"Sure," said Mr. Johnson. "You want to take a chance?"

The young man hesitated, looked longingly up the avenue toward what might have been his destination and then, when Mr. Johnson said "I'll pay for it" with his own peculiar convincing emphasis, turned and said, "Well, okay. But I got to see it first, what I'm buying."

Mr. Johnson, breathing hard, led the young man over to the side where the girl was standing; she had been watching with interest Mr. Johnson's capture of the young man and now, smiling timidly, she looked at Mr. Johnson as though prepared to be surprised at nothing.

Mr. Johnson reached into his pocket and took out his wallet. "Here," he said, and handed a bill to the girl. "This about equals your day's pay."

"But no," she said, surprised in spite of herself. "I mean, I couldn't."

"Please do not interrupt," Mr. Johnson told her. "And here," he said to the young man, "this will take care of you." The young man accepted the bill dazedly, but said, "Probably counterfeit" to the young woman out of the side of his mouth. "Now," Mr. Johnson went on, disregarding the young man, "what is your name, miss?"

"Kent," she said helplessly. "Mildred Kent."

"Fine," said Mr. Johnson. "And you, sir?"

"Arthur Adams," said the young man stiffly.

"Splendid," said Mr. Johnson. "Now, Miss Kent, I would like you to meet Mr. Adams. Mr. Adams, Miss Kent."

Miss Kent stared, wet her lips nervously, made a gesture as though she might run, and said, "How do you do?"

Mr. Adams straightened his shoulders, scowled at Mr. Johnson, made a gesture as though he might run, and said, "How do you do?"

"Now this," said Mr. Johnson, taking several bills from his wallet, "should be enough for the day for both of you. I would suggest perhaps a nice lunch somewhere, and dancing, or a matinee, or even a movie, although take care to choose a really good one; there are so many bad movies these days. You might," he said, struck with an inspiration, "visit the zoo, or the planetarium. Anywhere, as a matter of fact," he concluded, "that you would like to go. Have a nice time."

As he started to move away Arthur Adams, breaking from his dumbfounded stare, said, "But see here, mister, you can't do this. Why —how do you know—I mean, we don't even know—I mean, how do you know we won't just take the money and not do what you said?"

"You've taken the money," Mr. Johnson said. "You don't have to follow any of my suggestions. You may know something you prefer to do — perhaps a museum, or something."

"But suppose I just run away with it and leave her here?"

"I know you won't," said Mr. Johnson gently, "because you remembered to ask me that. Goodbye," he added, and went on.

As he stepped up the street, conscious of the sun on his head and his good shoes, he heard from somewhere behind him the young man saying, "Look, you know you don't have to if you don't want to," and the girl saying, "But unless you don't want to. . . ." Mr. Johnson smiled to himself and then thought that he had better hurry along; when he wanted to he could move very quickly, and before the young woman had gotten around to saying, "Well, I will if you will," Mr. Johnson was several blocks away and had already stopped twice, once to help a lady lift several large packages into a taxi and once to hand a peanut to a seagull. By this time he was in an area of large stores and many more people and he was buffeted constantly from either side by people hurrying and cross and late and sullen. Once he offered a peanut to a man who asked him for a dime, and once he offered a peanut to a bus driver who had stopped his bus at an intersection and had opened the window next to his seat and put out his head as though longing for fresh air and the comparative quiet of the traffic. The man wanting a dime took the peanut because Mr. Johnson had wrapped a dollar bill around it, but the bus driver took the peanut and asked ironically, "You want a transfer, Jack?"

On a busy corner Mr. Johnson encountered two young people—for one minute he thought they might be Mildred Kent and Arthur Adams—who were eagerly scanning a newspaper, their backs pressed against a storefront to avoid the people passing, their heads bent together. Mr. Johnson, whose curiosity was insatiable, leaned onto the storefront next to them and peeked over the man's shoulder; they were scanning the "Apartments Vacant" columns.

Mr. Johnson remembered the street where the woman and her little boy were going to Vermont and he tapped the man on the shoulder and said amiably, "Try down on West Seventeen. About the middle of the block, people moved out this morning."

"Say, what do you—," said the man, and then, seeing Mr. Johnson clearly, "Well, thanks. Where did you say?"

"West Seventeen," said Mr. Johnson. "About the middle of the block." He smiled again and said, "Good luck."

"Thanks," said the man.

"Thanks," said the girl, as they moved off.

"Goodbye," said Mr. Johnson.

He lunched alone in a pleasant restaurant, where the food was rich, and only Mr. Johnson's excellent digestion could encompass two of their whipped-cream-and-chocolate-and-rum-cake pastries for dessert. He had three cups of coffee, tipped the waiter largely, and went out into the street again into the wonderful sunlight, his shoes still comfortable and fresh on his feet. Outside he found a beggar staring into the windows of the restaurant he had left and, carefully looking through the money in his pocket, Mr. Johnson approached the beggar and pressed some coins and a couple of bills into his hand. "It's the price of the veal cutlet lunch plus tip," said Mr. Johnson. "Goodbye."

After his lunch he rested; he walked into the nearest park and fed peanuts to the pigeons. It was late afternoon by the time he was ready to start back downtown, and he had refereed two checker games and watched a small boy and girl whose mother had fallen asleep and awakened with surprise and fear which turned to amusement when she saw Mr. Johnson. He had given away almost all of his candy, and had fed all the rest of his peanuts to the pigeons, and it was time to go home. Although the late afternoon sun was pleasant, and his shoes were still entirely comfortable, he decided to take a taxi downtown.

He had a difficult time catching a taxi, because he gave up the first three or four empty ones to people who seemed to need them more; finally, however, he stood alone on the corner and — almost like netting a frisky fish — he hailed desperately until he succeeded in catching a cab which had been proceeding with haste uptown and seemed to draw in toward Mr. Johnson against its own will.

"Mister," the cab driver said as Mr. Johnson climbed in, "I figured you was an omen, like. I wasn't going to pick you up at all."

"Kind of you," said Mr. Johnson ambiguously.

"If I'd of let you go it would of cost me ten bucks," said the driver.

"Really?" said Mr. Johnson.

"Yeah," said the driver. "Guy just got out of the cab, he turned around and give me ten bucks, said take this and bet it in a hurry on a horse named Vulcan, right away."

"Vulcan?" said Mr. Johnson, horrified. "A fire sign on a Wednesday?"

"What?" said the driver. "Anyway, I said to myself if I got no fare between here and there I'd bet the ten, but if anyone looked like they needed the cab I'd take it as an omen and I'd take the ten home to the wife."

"You were very right," said Mr. Johnson heartily. "This is Wednesday, you would have lost your money. Monday, yes, or even Saturday. But never never never a fire sign on a Wednesday. Sunday would have been good, now."

"Vulcan don't run on Sunday," said the driver.

"You wait till another day," said Mr. Johnson. "Down this street, please, driver. I'll get off on the next corner."

"He told me Vulcan, though," said the driver.

"I'll tell you," said Mr. Johnson, hesitating with the door of the cab half open. "You take that ten dollars and I'll give you another ten dollars to go with it, and you go right ahead and bet that money on any Thursday on any horse that has a name indicating . . . let me see, Thursday . . . well, grain. Or any growing food."

"Grain?" said the driver. "You mean a horse named, like, Wheat or something?"

"Certainly," said Mr. Johnson. "Or, as a matter of fact, to make it even easier, any horse whose name includes the letters C, R, L.

Perfectly simple."

"Tall corn?" said the driver, a light in his eye. "You mean a horse named, like, Tall Corn?"

"Absolutely," said Mr. Johnson. "Here's your money."

"Tall Corn," said the driver. "Thank you, mister."

"Goodbye," said Mr. Johnson.

He was on his own corner and went straight up to his apartment. He let himself in and called "Hello?" and Mrs. Johnson answered from the kitchen, "Hello, dear, aren't you early?"

"Took a taxi home," Mr. Johnson said. "I remembered the cheesecake, too. What's for dinner?"

Mrs. Johnson came out of the kitchen and kissed him; she was a comfortable woman, and smiling as Mr. Johnson smiled. "Hard day?" she asked.

"Not very," said Mr. Johnson, hanging his coat in the closet. "How about you?"

"So-so," she said. She stood in the kitchen doorway while he settled into his easy chair and took off his good shoes and took out the paper he had bought that morning. "Here and there," she said.

"I didn't do so badly," Mr. Johnson said. "Couple young people."

"Fine," she said. "I had a little nap this afternoon, took it easy most of the day. Went into a department store this morning and accused the woman next to me of shoplifting, and had the store detective pick her up. Sent three dogs to the pound — you know, the usual thing. Oh, and listen," she added, remembering.

"What?" asked Mr. Johnson.

"Well," she said. "I got onto a bus and asked the driver for a transfer, and when he helped someone else first I said that he was impertinent, and quarreled with him. And then I said why wasn't he in the army, and I said it loud enough for everyone to hear, and I took his number and I turned in a complaint. Probably got him fired."

"Fine," said Mr. Johnson. "But you do look tired. Want to change over tomorrow?"

"I would like to," she said. "I could do with a change."

"Right," said Mr. Johnson. "What's for dinner?"

"Veal cutlet."

"Had it for lunch," said Mr. Johnson.

Suspense and Surprise

Tales of mystery, suspicion and terror fascinate us. The suspense writer creates a tension in us so that we must keep turning the pages to the very end to see how things work out. Why should we be attracted by mystery and terror? First, the situations described are usually "life or death". Anything *that* basic cannot help but grip our attention. Second, we are spectators who read the story, rather than participants in an actual event.

A writer uses tricks to arouse our interest. For example, he or she can slow the pace of the story by adding detail after detail. This has the same effect as holding the lid tightly on a pot of boiling water. The pressure builds dramatically. In all stories in this unit the writer builds suspense — withholding the final solution to the end.

Get set to travel into the magic world of mystery.

A Man Who Had No Eyes

MacKinlay Kantor

"And he gets out, and I lie there with all that poison gas pouring down on all sides of me. . . ."

A beggar was coming down the avenue just as Mr. Parsons emerged from his hotel.

He was a blind beggar, carrying the traditional battered cane, and thumping his way before him with the cautious, half-furtive effort of the sightless. He was a shaggy, thick-necked fellow; his coat was greasy about the lapels and pockets, and his hand splayed over the cane's crook with a futile sort of clinging. He wore a black pouch slung over his shoulder. Apparently he had something to sell.

The air was rich with spring; sun was warm and yellowed on the asphalt. Mr. Parsons, standing there in front of his hotel and noting the clack-clack approach of the sightless man, felt a sudden and foolish sort of pity for all blind creatures.

And, thought Mr. Parsons, he was very glad to be alive. A few years ago he had been little more than a skilled laborer; now he was successful, respected, admired . . . Insurance . . . And he had done it alone, unaided, struggling beneath handicaps . . . And he was still young. The blue air of spring, fresh from its memories of windy pools and lush shrubbery, could thrill him with eagerness.

He took a step forward just as the tap-tapping blind man passed him by. Quickly the shabby fellow turned.

"Listen, guv'nor. Just a minute of your time."

Mr. Parsons said, "It's late. I have an appointment. Do you want me to give you something?"

"I ain't no beggar, guv'nor. You bet I ain't. I got a handy little article here" — he fumbled until he could press a small object into Mr. Parsons' hand—"that I sell. One buck. Best cigarette lighter made."

Mr. Parsons stood there, somewhat annoyed and embarrassed. He was a handsome figure with his immaculate gray suit and gray hat and malacca stick. Of course the man with the cigarette lighters could not see him. . . .

"But I don't smoke," he said.

"Listen, I bet you know plenty people who smoke. Nice little present," wheedled the man. "And, mister, you wouldn't mind helping a poor guy out?" He clung to Mr. Parsons' sleeve.

Mr. Parsons sighed and felt in his vest pocket. He brought out two half dollars and pressed them into the man's hand. "Certainly I'll help you out. As you say, I can give it to someone. Maybe the elevator boy would —" He hesitated, not wishing to be boorish and inquisitive, even with a blind peddler. "Have you lost your sight entirely?"

The shabby man pocketed the two half dollars. "Fourteen years, guv'nor." Then he added with an insane sort of pride: "Westbury, sir, I was one of 'em."

"Westbury," repeated Mr. Parsons. "Ah, yes. The chemical explosion . . . The papers haven't mentioned it for years. But at the time it was supposed to be one of the greatest disasters in —"

"They've all forgot about it." The fellow shifted his feet wearily. "I tell you, guv'nor, a man who was in it don't forget about it. Last thing I ever saw was C shop going up in one grand smudge, and that damn' gas pouring in at all the busted windows."

Mr. Parsons coughed. But the blind peddler was caught up with the train of his one dramatic reminiscence. And, also, he was thinking that there might be more half dollars in Mr. Parsons' pocket.

"Just think about it, guv'nor. There was a hundred and eight people killed, about two hundred injured, and over fifty of them lost their eyes. Blind as bats —" He groped forward until his dirty hand rested against Mr. Parsons' coat. "I tell you sir, there wasn't nothing worse than that in the war. If I had lost my eyes in the war, okay. I would have been well took care of. But I was just a workman, working for what was in it. And I got it. You're damn' right I got it, while the capitalists were making their dough! They was insured, don't worry about that. They —"

"Insured," repeated his listener. "Yes. That's what I sell —"

"You want to know how I lost my eyes?" cried the man. "Well, here it is!" His words fell with the bitter and studied drama of a story often told, and told for money. "I was there in C shop, last of all the folks rushing out. Out in the air there was a chance, even with buildings exploding right and left. A lot of guys made it safe out the door and got away. And just when I was about there, crawling along between those big vats, a guy behind me grabs my leg. He says, 'Let me past, you—!' Maybe he was nuts. I dunno. I try to forgive him in my heart, guv'nor. But he was bigger than me. He hauls me back and climbs right over me! Tramples me into the dirt. And he gets out, and I lie there with all that poison gas pouring down on all sides of me, and flame and stuff . . ." He swallowed — a studied sob — and stood dumbly expectant. He could imagine the next words: *Tough luck, my man. Now, I want to —* "That's the story, guv'nor."

The spring wind shrilled past them, damp and quivering.

"Not quite," said Mr. Parsons.

The blind peddler shivered crazily. "Not quite? What you mean, you —?"

"The story is true," Mr. Parsons said, "except that it was the other way around."

"Other way around?" He croaked unamiably. "Say, guv'nor —"

"I was in C shop," said Mr. Parsons. "It was the other way around. You were the fellow who hauled back on me and climbed over me. You were bigger than I was, Markwardt."

The blind man stood for a long time, swallowing hoarsely. He gulped: "Parsons. By God. By God! I thought you —" And then he screamed fiendishly: "Yes. Maybe so. Maybe so. But I'm blind! I'm blind, and you've been standing here letting me spout to you, and laughing at me every minute! I'm blind!"

People in the street turned to stare at him.

"You got away, but I'm blind! Do you hear? I'm —"

"Well," said Mr. Parsons, "don't make such a row about it, Markwardt . . . So am I."

The Purple Children

Edith Pargeter

He hurtled after the racing boy, hauling the loaded spray-gun round from his shoulder in flight to bring it to bear upon the fugitive. He heard the girl scream. . . .

The outrage took place at eleven o'clock on a moonless night, before the stars began to silver the white walls of the church. It was the sentry at the rear gate of the Town Hall, an eighteen-year-old new to the town, who was singled out as the weakest spot in the defences. Half-dozing on his walk back and forth across the gate, he heard the most innocent sound in the world, a girl's voice calling softly: "Puss, puss, puss . . ."

As he started into wakefulness with the exaggerated attention which made the walls seem higher and the night darker, a little figure with the light running steps of a child darted towards the gate, and halted with her hands locked upon the bars. He saw how slight she was, and how young, no more than fifteen. Her frock was dark, probably black like so many of them here. She turned on him a face which was only a silvery oval and a dark shining of eyes, and he thought he saw about it the shadowy movement of unkempt locks darker than the darkness.

"You can't go in there," said the sentry gruffly. "You ought to be in the house at this time of night. Don't you know there's a curfew?"

"I *was* in the house. I only came out because of my cat; she got out when I went to bring in wood, and I couldn't catch her. She's young, she runs away. It's no use telling *her* there's a curfew."

"She'll come back in the morning," said the sentry awkwardly. "They always do. You go home like a good girl, and don't you risk running about here in the dark. Somebody might think you were up to something."

"But she might not come back. She's never been out at night before. I could get her now, if you'll let me. She ran through there into the courtyard. Won't you please help me to catch her?"

The boy felt the small, cold hand laid entreatingly upon his arm. She was only a kid, she hardly came up to his shoulder, and she was beginning to sniff ominously. He couldn't see any harm in it. He had orders to treat the natives politely and considerately, as long as they weren't making trouble, and what trouble could this waif possibly make?

"I can't! I should get into trouble if anybody found out . . ."

"Well, who's going to find out? All I want is to get my cat. You'll be there close to me every minute, you can see every move I make. And you've got a gun — I don't see what you have to be afraid of. Oh, do please help me!"

He hadn't meant to do it, but somehow he had set his hand to the bars beside hers, and thrust the gate open before her. "Well, be quiet about it, can't you, or somebody'll hear us. Come on, quick, and get her, and get yourself out of here."

She slipped past him like a shadow. He turned his back on the gate and the silent, dark lane outside and pressed at her shoulder as she flitted into the darkest corner of the yard, where the outhouses leaned together in a huddle of shadows, and the steps plunged down to the cellar. Behind them the tall bulk of the Town Hall shut off the awaking stars, and the ropes of the flagstaff creaked faintly in the wind which never stilled in the upper air.

"There she is!" whispered the girl triumphantly, and darted forward and was lost among the deeper shadows under the wall. And there really was a cat, the sentry saw with relief and satisfaction, a thin little tabby skipping from darkness to darkness, evading them with the light, unhurried insolence of cats everywhere. It took them ten minutes to run it to earth at the foot of the cellar steps, against the closed door. The girl snatched it up and held it struggling in her arms, and looked up at him under the black tangle of her hair with a wild smile.

"Thank you! Now I'll go home. You were very kind to let me come in!"

But she did not move; she stood looking at him still, her eyes enormous and shy and wary. When she looked at him like that he felt how alien he was in this place, and even her thanks could not compensate him for the quiet, patient hatred of her people. She let her body touch his, her sharp little shoulder leaning for a moment into the hollow of his arm, which moved of itself to hold her.

Then they both heard, clear through the silence, the sudden light impact of feet, as though someone had dropped from the high wall.

The sentry spun round and went up the cellar steps three at a time, just in time to see the figure of a boy disentangle itself from the severed ropes of the flagstaff, and run head-down for the gate.

The shout of rage and alarm was out of him before he knew it, and after that there was no hope of keeping it all quiet and pretending that no one had got past him during the night; the only chance he had was to get at least one prisoner to show for it. He hurtled after the racing boy, hauling the loaded spray-gun round from his shoulder in flight to bring it to bear upon the fugitive. He heard the girl scream, and was startled because the sound came from only a yard or two behind him, where silently, wildly, she was running, too. When she saw him check for an instant to steady the gun, she ran past him and flung the cat sprawling and clawing in his face.

He threw up his left arm to cover his eyes, and swerved aside, firing the gun blindly. The spray spattered darkly over her cheek and her spread hands, but she had gained the few yards she needed for herself and her partner, and she flew through the gate and pulled it to with a clang. Before the sentry could fling off the cat and wipe his eyes clear of the blood from his scratched forehead, both the fugitives were snatched away into the silence and darkness of the little streets.

People came pouring into the courtyard from three doors. They found the sentry mopping his face, a long, violet stain upon the ground, and the coils of severed rope dangling at the foot of the flagstaff. They got the major out of bed, and the sentry reported to him with every excuse he could think of, though the sum of them all sounded thin enough.

"She was only a kid about fifteen. I didn't think she could be up to anything, sir. She was looking for her cat."

The major had been in the country for over a year, and was accustomed to the local style of warfare, to the ugly demands it made upon him, and the satisfaction he sometimes felt in their ugliness, which frightened and depressed him more than anything else. He stood gazing at the boy without rancour.

"They're always kids of fifteen. Haven't you learned that yet?

"But there was a cat, sir, that was true, anyhow."

"That skinny tabby," said the major wearily, "belongs to the caretaker. I imagine its appearance was a stroke of luck. Or she may have seen it before she made up her story and began calling. Well, you seem to have spent practically a quarter of an hour being civil to her, I take it you can pick her out again?"

The sentry was too frightened of his own side, by this time, to retain much resentment against the enemy; his fear even drew him into a kind of distant alliance with them. He said: "No, sir, I don't think I could. It was pretty dark there under the wall. There's scores of them that same build, thin as a monkey."

"And scores of them with purple hands and faces? At least you had the sense to fire your charge. That ought to give her one distinguishing feature, don't you think?"

The sentry looked at the long dark stain like blood upon the stones, and was filled with a treasonable but unmistakable regret. "I'm sorry, sir," he lied. "It was just then she threw the cat, it put me off proper. I reckon I missed her."

"Then why," asked the major gently, "did she drip violet dye practically all the way to the gate?" He marked the last infinitesimal spot in the light of his torch. "A heavier charge, and we might have been able to follow her all the way home. Did you mark the boy, too?"

"No, sir. He was well out of range, only he turned back to catch hold of her hand." It was the first time he had fully realized all that he had seen. Regret rose in him like a tidal sea. "They haven't done anything all that bad, sir — it's only a flag!"

The major smiled. When this boy was forty instead of eighteen he would no longer make the absurd mistake of speaking of "only" a flag. "Whoever it was, he's left about ten feet of the flagstaff coiled round with barbed-wire as he came down. You must have been very absorbed in your cat-hunt. And he must have spent a long time practising the movements involved, before he could reproduce them at that speed. Yes, I should like to congratulate that boy! But when we've found her we shall have found him, too. We'll try the grammar school first," he said, smiling to himself, beginning to feel the terrifying satisfaction of hate reacting against hate. "If she isn't there, we'll look up the girls who don't answer the register. We shan't have to look any farther."

In the shed behind Pablito's father's shop Mariposa knelt over a pan of water, scouring with a handful of wet sand at the backs of her hands.

The water lay in her palms as she rinsed them as clear as it had come from the well. Juanito held the torch close, keeping his body between its light and the covered window. Teo crouched on his heels, his head bent close to Mariposa's, his cheek brushed occasionally by her swinging hair.

"It's no use," she said, letting her hands lie quiet in the wet skirt of her dress and looking up at him with enormous black eyes. The misshapen blotches of purple ate away half her face into shadow. Behind her all the silent, intent partisans drew closer with a long sigh. "It won't come out," she said with the calm of despair. "Now they have only to look for me—I can't be hidden. Teo, what am I to do?"

"If they find you," he said, taking her stained hands in his, "they find me, too."

"That's foolish! You'll be needed again. And besides, they'd beat you; they'll only imprison me. No, it was great luck that you were not splashed like me—don't be so ungrateful as to throw it away." But she was very frightened. He felt the small, wet hands, hot with scouring, tremble in his own.

"I will not let you bear it alone! We were all in this thing together. When we two drew the lots we drew the danger with them, as well as the privilege."

"They'll come straight to the school," said Juanito. "Perhaps if you stay at home and take care not to be seen..."

"For how long?" said Teo shortly. "You see the marks will have to wear away gradually. Do you think she can be hidden for months?"

"But they may give up in a week or two. She need not be hidden from our own people, only from *them*."

"If they do not find me in the school," said Mariposa with authority, "they will want to see the register and find out who is missing. It is only another way of being set apart. I think I would rather be there to face them. It is not I who will have cause to be ashamed." But her body shook and her hands contracted in the boy's hands, because she knew she would still be afraid.

"If we tried linen-bleach," said Luz timidly, "do you think it would move it?"

Esperanza shook her head. "It's an old vegetable dye, nothing will fetch it out, that's why all the dyers still use it. My father is a dyer," she said sadly. "I know!"

Teo stood up slowly, still holding the thin, marred hands in his. All the intent and anxious eyes settled upon him and clung hopefully, because he had begun to smile. He looked down and smiled into Mariposa's eyes, and his thin, brown face relaxed into a reassuring tranquility. "Come!" he said, drawing her up by the hands. "I have an idea! Come, all of you! It will be hours yet to daylight, we have a little time. Don't be afraid, they won't find you! They'll never find you!"

In the morning light the major looked out of his window and saw the silvery coils of new barbed-wire like a guardian serpent about the flagstaff, and above, afloat upon the restless wind, the expected flag, an enemy that could never be silenced. It would soon be down, of course. It could not be nailed to the staff, there had not been time, and silence had been essential. Yes, it would soon be down; the only trouble was that it would go up again somewhere else. It always did.

He had spent a year of his life searching the little houses of these towns for explosives and arms, for subversive literature in the native tongue, for wanted men on the run; but on every occasion the circumstances of the search became a little meaner, and more humiliating. Now it was a little girl with a face stained by vegetable dye, who had made a fool of a homesick boy and helped another boy to raise once again the ubiquitous flag. The major felt an impatience to have the miserable business finished; but by daylight he no longer mistook for anger and hatred what was, after all, nothing but disgust and exasperation.

The grammar school opened at eight o'clock; at half past eight the major presented himself there with a sergeant and two men.

He was punctilious in waiting in the entrance hall while the headmaster was fetched out to him.

"I need hardly tell you why I'm here," he said. "No doubt you've already seen the flag over the Town Hall. We intend to make an example this time. If you allow your children to move up into the front line, you must consider that it is you yourselves who inflict their punishments upon them. We would infinitely rather deal with you."

"We would infinitely rather that you did," agreed the headmaster, his spectacles a little askew on his antique and aquiline nose. "You must do what you feel to be your duty. But so must our children. Would you like to begin with the little ones? Forgive me, but your gambit leads me to suppose that you are looking for someone more than usually embarrassing as an opponent."

The major would have liked to think of a cutting reply, but the situation had placed irony clean out of his reach. "I am looking for a girl of about fifteen. You may not know that we have recently adopted the use of a spray-gun loaded with one of the local vegetable dyes. The girl will be stained purple. This time I can promise you there will be no collective punishments. This time it will not be necessary."

"Purple!" said the schoolmaster reflectively. "A royal colour. Also the colour of mourning. A nice choice!"

"There was also a boy, who will not be so immediately recognizable. But I think it hardly matters. Once we have our hands on the girl he will come forward of his own will."

"I see you have not entirely wasted your time with us," said the schoolmaster politely. "Very well! You wish to inspect our senior grades? I have kept them assembled in the hall for you. Please!"

The major strode across the polished lobby, the sergeant and his men keeping step behind him. The headmaster, advancing his hand to open the door, leveled one sudden, glittering glance into the eyes of the invader, and it seemed for an instant that what he felt for him was no longer simple antagonism, but almost pity. Then he pushed the door wide, and stood back for his visitors to enter.

The major marched over the threshold with the briskness of complete confidence, almost of triumph. Fifty-three young heads, with marvelous unanimity, were raised to confront him, the challenging light of fifty-three pairs of dark, wide, Byzantine eyes bristled at him like bayonets, and he checked in his stride and wrenched himself sidewise into stillness, as though he had indeed run his beribboned breast into a thicket of steel. He had come looking for a marked outcast. He beheld a regiment, a Pyrrhic phalanx of embattled children, all their delicate olive faces spattered from forehead to chin with the resplendent purple of royalty and mourning.

The Conger Eel

Liam O'Flaherty

Then he doubled back, rocking the boat as he
beat the sides with his whirling tail.

He was eight feet long. At the centre of his back he was two
feet in circumference. Slipping sinuously along the bottom of the sea
at a gigantic pace, his black, mysterious body glistened and twirled like
a wisp in a foaming cataract. His little eyes, stationed wide apart in his
flat-boned broad skull, searched the ocean for food. He coursed
ravenously for miles along the base of the range of cliffs. He searched
fruitlessly, except for three baby pollocks which he swallowed in one
mouthful without arresting his progress. He was very hungry.

Then he turned by a sharp promontory and entered a cliff-bound
harbour where the sea was dark and silent, shaded by the concave
cliffs. Savagely he looked ahead into the dark waters. Then instan-
taneously he flicked his tail, rippling his body like a twisted screw, and
shot forward. His long, thin, single whisker, hanging from his lower
snout like a label tag, jerked back under his belly. His glassy eyes rested
ferociously on minute white spots that scurried about in the sea a long
distance ahead. The conger eel had sighted his prey. There was a
school of mackerel a mile away.

He came upon them headlong, in a flash. He rose out of the deep from beneath their white bellies, and gripped one mackerel in his wide-open jaws ere his snout met the surface. Then, as if in a swoon, his body went limp, and tumbling over and over, convulsing like a crushed worm, he sank lower and lower until at last he had swallowed the fish. Then immediately he straightened out and flicked his tail, ready to pursue his prey afresh.

The school of mackerel, when the dread monster had appeared among them, were swimming just beneath the surface of the sea. When the eel rushed up they had hurled themselves clean out of the water with the sound of innumerable grains of sand being shaken up in an immense sieve. The thousand blue-and-white bodies flashed and shimmered in the sun for three moments, and then they disappeared, leaving a large patch of the dark water convulsing turbulently. Ten thousand little fins cut the surface of the sea as the mackerel set off in headlong flight. Their white bellies were no longer visible. They plunged down into the depths of the sea, where their blue-black sides and backs, the colour of the sea, hid them from their enemy. The eel surged about in immense figures of eight; but he had lost them.

Half hungry, half satisfied, he roamed about for an hour, a demented giant of the deep, travelling restlessly at an incredible speed. Then at last his little eyes again sighted his prey. Little white spots again hung like faded drops of brine in the sea ahead of him. He rushed thither. He opened his jaws as the spots assumed shape, and they loomed up close to his eyes. But just as he attempted to gobble the nearest one, he felt a savage impact. Then something hard and yet intangible pressed against his head and then down along his back. He leaped and turned. The hard, gripping material completely enveloped him. He was in a net. On all sides of him mackerel wriggled gasping in the meshes.

The eel paused for two seconds amazed and terrified. Then all around him he saw a web of black strands hanging miraculously in the water, everywhere, while mackerel with heaving gills stood rigid in the web, some with their tails and heads both caught and their bodies curved in an arch, others encompassed many times in the uneven folds, others girdled firmly below the gills with a single black thread. Glittering, they eddied back and forth with the stream of the sea, a mass of fish being strangled in the deep.

Then the eel began to struggle fiercely to escape. He hurtled hither and thither, swinging his long slippery body backwards and forwards, ripping with his snout, surging forward suddenly at full speed, churning the water. He ripped and tore the net, cutting great long gashes in it. But the more he cut and ripped the more deeply enmeshed did he become. He did not release himself, but he released some of the mackerel. They fell from the torn meshes, stiff and crippled, downwards, sinking like dead things. Then suddenly one after the other they seemed to wake from sleep, shook their tails, and darted away, while the giant eel was gathering coil upon coil of the net about his slippery body. Then, at last, exhausted and half strangled, he lay still, heaving.

Presently he felt himself being hauled up in the net. The net crowded around him more, so that the little gleaming mackerel, imprisoned with him, rubbed his sides and lay soft and flabby against him all hauled up in the net with him. He reached the surface and gasped, but he made no movement. Then he was hauled into a boat, and fell with a thud into the bottom.

The two fishermen in the boat began to curse violently when they saw the monstrous eel that had torn their net and ruined their catch of mackerel. The old man on the oars and bow called out: "Free him and kill him." The young man who was hauling in the net looked in terror at the slippery monster that lay between his feet, with its little eyes looking up cunningly, as if it were human. He almost trembled as he picked up the net and began to undo the coils. "Slash it with your knife," yelled the old man, "before he does more harm." The young man picked up his knife from the gunwale where it was stuck, and cut the net, freeing the eel. The eel, with a sudden and amazing movement, glided up the bottom of the boat, so that he stretched full length.

Then he doubled back, rocking the boat as he beat the sides with his whirling tail, his belly flopping in the water that lay in the bottom. The two men screamed, both crying: "Kill him, or he'll drown us." "Strike him!" They both reached for the short, thick stick that hung from a peg amidships. The young man grabbed it, bent down, and struck at the eel. "Hit him!" cried the old man; "catch him, catch him, and turn him over."

They both bent down, pawing at the eel, cursing and panting, while the boat rocked ominously and the huge conger eel glided around and around at an amazing speed. Their hands clawed his sides, slipping over them like skates on ice. They gripped him with their knees, they stood on him, they tried to lie on him, but in their confusion they could not catch him.

Then at last the young man lifted him in his arms, holding him in the middle, gripping him as if he were trying to crush him. He staggered upwards. "Now strike him!" he yelled to the old man. But suddenly he staggered backwards. The boat rocked. He dropped the eel with an oath, reaching out with his hands to steady himself. The eel's head fell over the canted gunwale. His snout dipped into the sea. With an immense shiver he glided away, straight down, down to the depths, down like an arrow, until he reached the dark, weed-covered rocks at the bottom.

Then stretching out to his full length he coursed in a wide arc to his enormous lair, far away in the silent depths.

Through the Tunnel

Doris Lessing

Something soft and clammy touched his mouth. He saw a
dark frond moving against the grayish rock and panic
filled him. He thought of octopuses, or clinging weed.

Going to the shore on the first morning of the holiday, the
young English boy stopped at a turning of the path and looked down at
a wild and rocky bay, and then over to the crowded beach he knew
so well from other years. His mother walked in front of him, carrying
a bright striped bag in one hand. Her other arm, swinging loose, was
very white in the sun.

The boy watched that white, naked arm, and turned his eyes, which
had a frown behind them, toward the bay and back again to his
mother. When she felt he was not with her, she swung around.

"Oh, there you are, Jerry!" she said. She looked impatient, then
smiled. "Why, darling, would you rather not come with me? Would
you rather —" She frowned, conscientiously worrying over what
amusements he might secretly be longing for which she had been
too busy to imagine.

He was very familiar with that anxious, apologetic smile. Contrition sent him running after her. And yet, as he ran, he looked back
over his shoulder at the wild bay; and all morning, as he played on the
safe beach, he was thinking of it.

Next morning, when it was time for the routine of swimming and
sunbathing, his mother said, "Are you tired of the usual beach, Jerry?
Would you like to go somewhere else?"

"Oh, no!" he said quickly, smiling at her out of that unfailing
impulse of contrition—a sort of chivalry. Yet, walking down the path
with her, he blurted out, "I'd like to go and have a look at those rocks
down there."

She gave the idea her attention. It was a wild-looking place, and there was no one there, but she said, "Of course, Jerry. When you've had enough, come to the big beach. Or just go straight back to the villa, if you like."

She walked away, that bare arm, now slightly reddened from yesterday's sun, swinging. And he almost ran after her again, feeling it unbearable that she should go by herself, but he did not.

She was thinking. Of course he's old enough to be safe without me. Have I been keeping him too close? He mustn't feel he ought to be with me. I must be careful.

He was an only child, eleven years old. She was a widow. She was determined to be neither possessive nor lacking in devotion. She went worrying off to her beach.

As for Jerry, once he saw that his mother had gained her beach, he began the steep descent to the bay. From where he was, high up among red-brown rocks, it was a scoop of moving bluish green fringed with white.

As he went lower, he saw that it spread among small promontories and inlets of rough, sharp rock, and the crisping, lapping surface showed stains of purple and darker blue. Finally, as he ran sliding and scraping down the last few yards, he saw an edge of white surf, and the shallow, luminous movement of water over white sand, and, beyond that, a solid, heavy blue.

He ran straight into the water and began swimming. He was a good swimmer. He went out fast over the gleaming sand, over a middle region where rocks lay like discoloured monsters under the surface, and then he was in the real sea — a warm sea where irregular cold currents from the deep water shocked his limbs.

When he was so far out that he could look back not only on the little bay but past the promontory that was between it and the big beach, he floated on the buoyant surface and looked for his mother. There she was, a speck of yellow under an umbrella that looked like a slice of orange peel. He swam back to shore, relieved at being sure she was there, but all at once very lonely.

On the edge of a small cape that marked the side of the bay away from the promontory was a loose scatter of rocks. Above them, some boys were stripping off their clothes. They came running, naked, down to the rocks.

The English boy swam towards them, and kept his distance at a stone's throw. They were of that coast, all of them burned smooth dark brown, and speaking a language he did not understand. To be with them, of them, was a craving that filled his whole body. He swam a little closer; they turned and watched him with narrowed, alert dark eyes.

Then one smiled, and waved. It was enough. In a minute, he had swum in and was on the rocks beside them, smiling with a desperate, nervous supplication. They shouted cheerful greetings at him, and though they observed his nervous, uncomprehending smile, they understood that he was a foreigner strayed from his own beach and they proceeded to forget him. But he was happy. He was with them.

They began diving again and again from a high point into a well of blue sea between rough, pointed rocks. After they had dived and come up, they swam around, hauled themselves up, and waited their turn to dive again.

They were big boys — men to Jerry. He dived, and they watched him, and when he swam around to take his place, they made way for him. He felt he was accepted, and he dived again carefully, proud of himself.

Soon the biggest of the boys poised himself, shot down into the water, and did not come up. The others stood about watching. Jerry, after waiting for the sleek brown head to appear, let out a yell of warning; they looked at him idly and turned their eyes back toward the water.

After a long time, the boy came up on the other side of a big dark rock, letting the air out of his lungs in a sputtering gasp and a shout of triumph. Immediately, the rest of them dived in. One moment, the morning seemed full of chattering boys; the next, the air and the surface of the water were empty. But through the heavy blue, dark shapes could be seen moving and groping.

Jerry dived, shot past the school of underwater swimmers, saw a black wall of rock looming at him, touched it, and bobbed up at once to the surface, where the wall was a low barrier he could see across. There was no one visible; under him, in the water, the dim shapes of the swimmers had disappeared. Then one, and then another of the boys came up on the far side of the barrier of rock, and he understood that they had swum through some gap or hole in it. He plunged down again.

He could see nothing through the stinging salt water but the blank rock. When he came up, the boys were all on the diving rock, preparing to attempt the feat again. And now, in a panic of failure, he yelled up, in English, "Look at me! Look!" and he began splashing and kicking in the water like a foolish dog.

They looked down gravely, frowning. He knew the frown. At moments of failure, when he clowned to claim his mother's attention, it was with just this grave embarrassed inspection that she rewarded him.

Through his hot shame, feeling the pleading grin on his face like a scar that he could never remove, he looked up at the group of big brown boys on the rock and shouted *"Bonjour! Merci! Au revoir! Monsieur, monsieur!"* while he hooked his fingers round his ears and waggled them.

Water surged into his mouth; he choked, sank, came up. The rock, lately weighted with the boys, seemed to rear up out of the water as their weight was removed. They were flying down past him, now, into the water; the air was full of falling bodies. Then the rock was empty in the hot sunlight. He counted one, two three . . .

At fifty, he was terrified. They must all be drowning beneath him, in the watery caves of the rock! At a hundred, he stared around him at the empty hillside, wondering if he should yell for help.

He counted faster, faster, to hurry them up, to bring them to the surface quickly, to drown them quickly — anything rather than the terror of counting on and on into the blue emptiness of the morning. And then, at a hundred and sixty, the water beyond the rock was full of boys blowing like brown whales. They swam back to the shore without a look at him.

He climbed back to the diving rock and sat down, feeling the hot roughness of it under his thighs. The boys were gathering up their bits of clothing and running off along the shore to another promontory.

They were leaving to get away from him. He cried openly, his fists in his eyes. There was no one to see him, and he cried himself out.

It seemed to him that a long time had passed and he swam out to where he could see his mother. Yes, she was still there, a yellow spot under an orange umbrella. He swam back to the big rock, climbed up, and dived into the blue pool among the fanged and angry boulders. Down he went, until he touched the wall of rock again. But the salt was so painful in his eyes that he could not see.

He came to the surface, swam to shore, and went back to the villa to wait for his mother. Soon she walked slowly up the path, swinging her striped bag, the blushed, naked arm dangling beside her. "I want some swimming goggles," he panted, defiant and beseeching.

She gave him a patient, inquisitive look as she said casually, "Well, of course, darling."

But now, now, now! He must have them this minute and no other time. He nagged and pestered until she went with him to a shop. As soon as she had bought the goggles, he grabbed them from her hand as if she were going to claim them for herself, and was off, running down the steep path to the bay.

Jerry swam out to the big barrier rock, adjusted the goggles, and dived. The impact of the water broke the rubber-enclosed vacuum, and the goggles came loose.

He understood that he must swim down to the base of the rock from the surface of the water. He fixed the goggles tight and firm, filled his lungs, and floated, face down on the water.

Now he could see. It was as if he had eyes of a different kind — fish-eyes that showed everything clear and delicate and wavering in the bright water.

Under him, six or seven feet down, was a floor of perfectly clean, shining white sand, rippled firm and hard by the tides. Two grayish shapes steered there, like long, rounded pieces of wood or slate.

They were fish. He saw them nose toward each other, poise motionless, make a dart forward, swerve off, and come around again. It was like a water dance.

A few inches above them, the water sparkled as if sequins were dropping through it. Fish again — myriads of minute fish, the length of his fingernail, were drifting through the water, and in a moment he could feel the innumerable tiny touches of them, against his limbs. It was like swimming in flaked silver.

The great rock the big boys had swum through rose sheer out of the white sand, black, tufted lightly with greenish weed. He could see no gap in it. He swam down to its base.

Again and again he rose, took a big chestful of air, and went down. Again and again he groped over the surface of the rock, feeling it, almost hugging it in the desperate need to find the entrance.

And then, once, while he was clinging to the black wall, his knees came up and he shot his feet out forward and they met no obstacle.

He had found the hole.

He gained the surface, clambered about the stones that littered the barrier rock until he found a big one, and, with this in his arms, let himself down over the side of the rock. He dropped, with the weight, to the sandy floor.

Clinging tight to the anchor of the stone, he lay on his side and looked in under the dark shelf at the place where his feet had gone. He could see the hole.

It was an irregular, dark gap, but he could not see deep into it. He let go of his anchor, clung with his hands to the edges of the hole, and tried to push himself in.

He got his head in, found his shoulders jammed, moved them in sidewise, and was inside as far as his waist. He could see nothing ahead.

Something soft and clammy touched his mouth. He saw a dark frond moving against the grayish rock, and panic filled him. He thought of octopuses, or clinging weed.

He pushed himself out backward and caught a glimpse, as he retreated, of a harmless tentacle of seaweed drifting in the mouth of the tunnel. But it was enough.

He reached the sunlight, swam to shore, and lay on the diving rock. He looked down into the blue well of water. He knew he must find his way through that cave, or hole, or tunnel, and out the other side.

First, he thought, he must learn to control his breathing. He let himself down into the water with another big stone in his arms, so that he could lie effortlessly on the bottom.

One, two, three. He counted steadily. He could hear the movement of blood in his head. Fifty-one, fifty-two . . .

His chest was hurting. He let go of the rock and went up into the air. He saw that the sun was low. He rushed to the villa and found his mother at her supper. She said only, "Did you enjoy yourself?" and he said, "Yes." All night, the boy dreamed of the water-filled cave in the rock, and as soon as breakfast was over he went to the bay.

That night, his nose bled badly. For hours he had been underwater, learning to hold his breath, and now he felt weak and dizzy. His mother said, "I shouldn't overdo things, darling, if I were you."

That day and the next, Jerry exercised his lungs as if everything, the whole of his life, all that he would become, depended upon it. Again his nose bled at night, and his mother insisted on his coming with her the next day.

It was a torment to him to waste a day of his careful self-training, but he stayed with her on that other beach, which now seemed a place for small children, a place where his mother might lie safe in the sun. It was not his beach.

He did not ask for permission, on the following day, to go to his beach. He went, before his mother could consider the complicated rights and wrongs of the matter.

A day's rest, he discovered, had improved his count by ten. The big boys had made the passage while he counted a hundred and sixty. He had been counting fast, in his fright. Probably now, if he tried, he could get through that long tunnel, but he was not going to try yet.

A curious, most unchildlike persistence, a controlled impatience, made him wait. In the meantime, he lay under-water on the white sand, littered now by stones he had brought down from the upper air, and studied the entrance to the tunnel. He knew every jut and corner of it, as far as it was possible to see. It was as if he already felt its sharpness about his shoulders.

He sat by the clock in the villa, when his mother was not near, and checked his time. He was incredulous and then proud to find he could hold his breath without strain for two minutes. The words 'two minutes', authorized by the clock, brought the adventure that was so necessary to him close.

In another four days, his mother said casually one morning, they must go home. On the day before they left, he would do it. He would do it if it killed him, he said defiantly to himself. But two days before they were to leave — a day of triumph when he increased his count by fifteen — his nose bled so badly that he turned dizzy and had to lie limply over the big rock like a bit of seaweed, watching the thick red blood flow onto the rock and trickle slowly down to the sea. He was frightened.

Supposing he turned dizzy in the tunnel? Supposing he died there, trapped? Supposing — his head went around in the hot sun, and he almost gave up. He thought he would return to the house and lie down, and next summer, perhaps, when he had another year's growth in him — then he would go through the hole.

But even after he had made the decision, or thought he had, he found himself sitting up on the rock and looking down into the water, and he knew that now, this moment when his nose had only just stopped bleeding, when his head was still sore and throbbing — this was the moment when he would try. If he did not do it now, he never would.

He was trembling with fear that he would not go, and he was trembling with horror at that long, long tunnel under the rock, under the sea. Even in the open sunlight, the barrier rock seemed very wide and very heavy; tons of rock pressed down on where he would go. If he died there he would lie until one day—perhaps not before next year — those big boys would swim into it and find it blocked.

He put on his goggles, fitted them tight, tested the vacuum. His hands were shaking. Then he chose the biggest stone he could carry and slipped over the edge of the rock until half of him was in the cool, enclosing water and half in the hot sun.

He looked up once at the empty sky, filled his lungs once, twice, and then sank fast to the bottom with the stone. He let it go and began to count. He took the edges of the hole in his hands and drew himself into it, wriggling his shoulders in sidewise as he remembered he must.

Soon he was clear inside. He was in a small rock-bound hole filled with yellowish-gray water. The water was pushing him up against the roof. The roof was sharp and pained his back. He pulled himself along with his hands — fast, fast — and used his legs as levers.

His head knocked against something; a sharp pain dizzied him. Fifty, fifty-one, fifty-two . . . He was without light, and the water seemed to press upon him with the weight of rock. Seventy-one, seventy-two . . . There was no strain on his lungs. He felt like an inflated balloon, his lungs were so light and easy, but his head was pulsing.

He was being continually pressed against the sharp roof which felt slimy as well as sharp. Again, he thought of octopuses, and wondered if the tunnel might be filled with weed and could tangle him. He gave himself a panicky, convulsive kick forward, ducked his head, and swam.

His feet and hands moved freely, as if in open water. The hole must have widened out. He thought he must be swimming fast, and he was frightened of banging his head if the tunnel narrowed.

A hundred, a hundred and one . . . The water paled. Victory filled him. His lungs were beginning to hurt. A few more strokes and he would be out. He was counting wildly; he said a hundred and fifteen, and then, a long time later, a hundred and fifteen again. The water was a clear jewel-green all around him. Then he saw, above his head, a crack running up through the rock. Sunlight was falling through it, showing the clean dark rock of the tunnel, a single mussel shell, and darkness ahead.

He was at the end of what he could do. He looked up at the crack as if it were filled with air and not water, as if he could put his mouth to it to draw in air. A hundred and fifteen, he heard himself say inside his head — but he had said that long ago.

He must go on into the blackness ahead, or he would drown. His head was swelling, his lungs cracking. A hundred and fifteen, a hundred and fifteen pounded through his head, and he feebly clutched at rocks in the dark, pulling himself forward, leaving the brief space of sunlit water behind.

He felt he was dying. He was no longer quite conscious. He struggled on in the darkness between lapses into unconsciousness. An immense, swelling pain filled his head, and then the darkness cracked with an explosion of green light. His hands, groping forward, met nothing, and his feet, kicking back, propelled him out into the open sea.

He drifted to the surface, his face turned up to the air. He was gasping like a fish. He felt he would sink now and drown; he could not swim the few feet back to the rock. Then he was clutching it and pulling himself up onto it.

He lay face down, gasping. He could see nothing but a red-veined, clotted dark. His eyes must have burst, he thought; they were full of blood. He tore off the goggles and a gout of blood went into the sea. His nose was bleeding, and the blood had filled the goggles.

He scooped up handfuls of water from the cool, salty sea, to splash on his face, and did not know whether it was blood or salt water he tasted. After a time, his heart quieted, his eyes cleared, and he sat up.

He could see the local boys diving and playing half a mile away. He did not want them. He wanted nothing but to get back home and lie down.

In a short while, Jerry swam to shore and climbed slowly up the path to the villa. He flung himself on his bed and slept, waking at the sound of feet on the path outside. His mother was coming back. He rushed to the bathroom, thinking she must not see his face with bloodstains, or tearstains, on it. He came out of the bathroom and met her as she walked into the villa.

"Have a nice morning?" she asked, laying her hand on his warm brown shoulder a moment.

"Oh, yes, thank you," he said.

"You look a bit pale," And then, sharp and anxious, "How did you bang your head?"

"Oh, just banged it," he told her.

She looked at him closely. He was strained. His eyes were glazed looking. She was worried. And then she said to herself, "Oh, don't fuss! Nothing can happen. He can swim like a fish."

They sat down to lunch together.

"Mummy," he said, "I can stay under water for two minutes—three minutes, at least." It came bursting out of him.

"Can you, darling?" she said. "Well, I shouldn't overdo it. I don't think you ought to swim any more today."

She was ready for a battle of wills, but he gave in at once. It was no longer of the least importance to go to the bay.

Clerical Error

James Gould Cozzens

Mr. Joreth slid agilely from his seat, caught the telephone off the desk, kicking a chair into the colonel's path.

There were three steps down from the street door. Then the store extended, narrow and low between the book-packed walls, sixty or seventy feet to a little cubby-hole of an office where a large sallow man worked under a shaded desk-lamp. He had heard the street door open, and he looked that way a moment, peering intently through his spectacles. Seeing only a thin, stiffly erect gentleman with a small cropped white moustache, standing hesitant before the table with the sign Any Book 50 Cents, he returned to the folded copy of a religious weekly on the desk in front of him. He looked at the obituary column again, pulled a pad toward him and made a note. When he had finished, he saw, upon looking up again, that the gentleman with the white moustache had come all the way down the store.

"Yes, sir?" he said, pushing the papers aside. "What can I do for you?"

The gentleman with the white moustache stared at him keenly. "I am addressing the proprietor, Mr. Joreth?" he said.

"Yes, sir. You are."

"Quite so. My name is Ingalls — Colonel Ingalls."

"I'm glad to know you, Colonel. What can I —"

"I see that the name does not mean anything to you."

Mr. Joreth took off his spectacles, looked searchingly. "Why, no, sir. I am afraid not. Ingalls. No. I don't know anyone by that name."

Colonel Ingalls thrust his stick under his arm and drew an envelope from his inner pocket. He took a sheet of paper from it, unfolded the sheet, scowled at it a moment, and tossed it onto the desk. "Perhaps," he said. "this will refresh your memory."

Mr. Joreth pulled his nose a moment, looked harder at Colonel Ingalls, replaced his spectacles. "Oh," he said, "a bill. Yes. You must excuse me. I do much of my business by mail with people I've never met personally. 'The Reverend Doctor Godfrey Ingalls, Saint John's Rectory.' Ah, yes, yes —"

"The late Doctor Ingalls was my brother. This bill is obviously an error. He would never have ordered, received, or wished to read any of these works. Naturally, no such volumes were found among his effects."

"Hm," said Mr. Joreth. "Yes, I see." He read down the itemized list, coughed, as though in embarrassment. "I see. Now, let me check my records a moment." He dragged down a vast battered folio from the shelf behind him. "G, H, I —," he muttered. "Ingalls. Ah, now —"

"There is no necessity for that," said Colonel Ingalls. "It is, of course, a mistake. A strange one, it seems to me. I advise you strongly to be more careful. If you choose to debase yourself by surreptitiously selling works of the sort, that is your business. But —"

Mr. Joreth nodded several times, leaned back. "Well, Colonel," he said, "you're entitled to your opinion. I don't sit in judgment on the tastes of my customers. Now, in this case, there seems unquestionably to have been an order for the books noted from the source indicated. On the fifteenth of last May I filled the order. Presumably they arrived. What became of them then, is no affair of mine; but in view of your imputation, I might point out that such literature is likely to be kept in a private place and read privately. For eight succcessive months I sent a statement. I have never received payment. Of course, I was unaware that the customer was, didn't you say, deceased. Hence my reference to legal action on this last. I'm very sorry to have —"

"You unmitigated scoundrel!" roared Colonel Ingalls. "Do you really mean definitely to maintain that Doctor Ingalls purchased such books? Let me tell you —"

Mr. Joreth said: "My dear sir, one moment, if you please! Are you in a position to be so positive? I imply nothing about the purchaser.

I mean to maintain nothing, except that I furnished goods, for which I am entitled to payment. I am a poor man. When people do not pay me, what can I do but —"

"Why, you infamous —"

Mr. Joreth held up his hand. "Please, please!" he protested. "I think you are taking a most unjust and unjustified attitude, Colonel. This account has run a long while. I've taken no action. I am well aware of the unpleasantness which would be caused for many customers if a bill for books of this sort was made public. The circumstances aren't by any means unique, my dear sir; a list of my confidential customers would no doubt surprise you."

Colonel Ingalls said carefully: "Be good enough to show me my brother's original order."

"Ah," said Mr. Joreth. He pursed his lips. "That's unfair of you, Colonel. You are quite able to see that I wouldn't have it. It would be the utmost imprudence for me to keep on file anything which could cause so much trouble. I have the carbon of an invoice, which is legally sufficient, under the circumstances, I think. You see my position."

"Clearly," said Colonel Ingalls. "It is the position of a dirty knave and a blackguard, and I shall give myself the satisfaction of thrashing you." He whipped the stick from under his arm. Mr. Joreth slid agilely from his seat, caught the telephone off the desk, kicking a chair into the colonel's path.

"Operator," he said, "I want a policeman." Then he jerked open a drawer, plucked a revolver from it. "Now, my good sir," he said, his back against the wall, "we shall soon see. I have put up with a great deal of abuse from you, but there are limits. To a degree I understand your provocation, though it doesn't excuse your conduct. If you choose to take yourself out of here at once and send me a check for the amount due me, we will say no more."

Colonel Ingalls held the stick tight in his hand. "I think I will wait for the officer," he said with surprising composure. "I was too hasty. In view of your list of so-called customers, which you think would surprise me, there are doubtless other people to be considered —"

The stick in his hand leaped, sudden and slashing, catching Mr. Joreth over the wrist. The revolver flew free, clattered along the floor, and Colonel Ingalls kicked it behind him. "It isn't the sort of thing the relatives of a clergyman would like to have made public, is it? When you read of the death of one, what is to keep you from sending a bill?

Very often they must pay and shut up. A most ingenious scheme, sir."

Mr. Joreth clasped his wrist, wincing. "I am at loss to understand this nonsense," he said. "How dare you —"

"Indeed?" said Colonel Ingalls. "Ordinarily I might be at loss myself, sir; but in this case I think you put your foot in it, sir! I happen to be certain that my late brother ordered no books from you, that he did not keep them in private or read them in private. It was doubtless not mentioned in the obituary, but for fifteen years previous to his death Doctor Ingalls had the misfortune to be totally blind . . . . There, sir, is the policeman you sent for."

Tears and Triumph

The area of human feelings is the most sensitive that writers can explore. Stories about our emotions touch us all.

The people who inhabit the stories we read may not react as we would in particular situations. For example, they might show fear where we would show fearlessness. Still we understand their terror because we, too, have had similar feelings in different circumstances. Writers tell of our individual differences, but at the same time they show us the common humanity of all people.

The writer closes the gaps not just between our generation and the next, but through all of human history. We discover that people in the 13th century had the same feelings and reacted in the same way — blushed, laughed, got sick, became angry — as people did in the 17th century, or the 19th, or today. Feelings are ageless . . . timeless.

However, we also see people at cross-purposes with one another, people in conflict because they do not or cannot communicate their feelings. We see that pain and struggle often arise because people refuse, for one reason or another, to admit a common humanity.

Finally, the writer shows how people cope with events and problems. Human success or failure is measured, for the most part, by how well the characters handle their difficulties. Many of the stories which capture us with their magic are about people striving to overcome great odds. We are attracted to such stories because that's what we want for ourselves.

From Mother... With Love

Zoa Sherburne

Her mother was going to die.
Her mother. To die, the doctor said.

It began like any other Saturday, with Minta lying in bed an extra hour. Breakfast was always lazy and unhurried on Saturday mornings. The three of them in the breakfast room — Minta's father engrossed in his paper; her mother flying around in a gayly colored housecoat, mixing waffles and frying bacon; Minta setting the table.

They talked, the casual happy talk of people who love each other and don't have to make conversation. About neighborhood doings . . . about items in the paper . . . about the clothes Minta would need when she went to school in a couple of weeks.

It was after the dishes were finished that Minta's father asked her if she would like to go down to the beach for a little while. They started walking up the beach slowly, not toward the group of people digging clams, but in the other direction, toward the jagged pile of rocks that jutted out into the bay.

She heard a strange voice, her own voice.

"I thought . . . I thought you wanted to talk to me about school, but it isn't that, is it, Father?"

His fingers tightened around hers. "In a way it is . . . about school."

And then, before the feeling of relief could erase the fear, he went on. "I went to see Dr. Morton last week, Minta. I've been seeing him pretty regularly these last few months."

She flashed a quick frightened look up at him. "You aren't ill?"

"No." He sighed and it was a heartbreaking sound. "No. It isn't me. It's your mother."

She broke off and stopped walking and her hand was steady on his arm. "Tell me," she said quietly.

The look was back in his eyes again but this time Minta scarcely noticed it. She was aware only of his words, the dreadful echoing finality of his words.

Her mother was going to die.

Her mother.

To die, the doctor said. Three months, perhaps less . . .

Her mother who was scatterbrained and more fun than anyone else in the world. Her mother who could be counted on to announce in the spring, that she was going to do her Christmas shopping early this year, and then would leave everything until the week before Christmas.

She wasn't ever sick — except for the headaches and the operation last year which she had laughingly dismissed as a rest cure.

"I shouldn't have told you." Her father was speaking in a voice that Minta had never heard from him before.

"Of course you had to tell me." she said steadily. "Of course I had to know." And then — "Three months, but Dad, that's Christmas."

He took her hand and tucked it under his arm and they started walking again.

Just before they reached home he reached over and took her hand in a tight hurting grip.

"We can't tell her, Minta. The doctor left it up to me and I said not to tell her. We have to let her have this last time . . . this last little time . . . without that hanging over her. We have to go on as if everything were exactly the same."

It seemed impossible that life could go on exactly as before but Minta and her father knew that they must try.

The small private world peopled by the three of them was kept as snug and warm and happy as though no shadow had touched them.

They watched television and argued good-naturedly about the programs. Minta's friends came and went and there was the usual round of parties and dances and games. Her father continued to bowl two evenings a week and her mother became involved in various pre-holiday pursuits.

"I really must get at my Christmas shopping," she mentioned the day she was wrapping trick-or-treat candy for Halloween.

Minta shook her head and sighed gustily.

Her mother started this "I must-get-at-my-Christmas-shopping" routine every spring, but she never actually got around to it until two or three days before Christmas.

It was amazing that Minta could laugh and say, "Oh, you . . ." the way she did year after year.

That night she wakened in the chilly darkness of her room and began to cry softly, her head buried in the curve of her arm. At first it helped, loosening the tight bands about her heart, washing away the fear and the loneliness, but when she tried to stop she found that she couldn't. Great wracking sobs shook her until she could no longer smother them against her pillow. And then the light was on and her mother was there bending over her, her face concerned, her voice soothing.

"Darling, what is it? Wake up, baby, you're having a bad dream."

"No . . . no, it isn't a dream," Minta choked. "It's true . . . it's true."

The thin hand kept smoothing back her tumbled hair and her mother went on talking in the tone she had always used to comfort a much smaller Minta.

She was aware that her father had come to the doorway. He said nothing, just stood there watching them while Minta's sobs diminished into hiccupy sighs.

Her mother pulled the blanket up over Minta's shoulder and gave her a little spank. "The idea! Gremlins, at your age," she said reprovingly. "Want me to leave the light on in case your spook comes back?"

Minta shook her head, blinking against the tears that crowded against her eyelids, even managing a smile.

She never cried again.

Not even when the ambulance came a week later to take her mother to the hospital. Not even when she was standing beside her mother's high white hospital bed, holding her hand tightly, forcing herself to chatter of inconsequential things.

"Be sure that your father takes his vitamin pills, won't you, Minta? He's so careless unless I'm there to keep an eye on him."

"I'll watch him like a beagle," Minta promised lightly. "Now you behave yourself and get out of here in a hurry, you hear?"

Not even at the funeral . . .

The friends and relatives came and went and it was as if she stood on the sidelines watching the Minta who talked with them and answered their questions. As if her heart were encased in a shell that kept it from breaking.

She went to school and came home afterwards to the empty house. She tried to do the things her mother had done but even with the help of well-meaning friends and neighbors it was hard. She tried not to hate the people who urged her to cry.

"You'll feel better, dear," her Aunt Grace had insisted and then had lifted her handkerchief to her eyes and walked away when Minta had only stared at her with chilling indifference.

She overheard people talking about her mother.

"She never knew, did she?" they asked.

And always Minta's father answered, "No, she never knew. Even at the very last, when she was waiting for the ambulance to come she looked around the bedroom and said, 'I must get these curtains done up before Christmas.' "

One night Minta's father came to the door of her room where she was studying.

"I wonder if you'd like to go through those clothes before your Aunt Grace takes them to the church bazaar," he began haltingly. And then when she looked up at him, not understanding, he went on gently, "Your mother's clothes. We thought someone might as well get some good out of them."

She stood up and closed the book and went past him without another word, but she closed the door behind her when she went into her mother's room.

At the very back of the closet were the two pieces of matched luggage that had been her mother's last birthday gift from her father. They were heavy when she tried to move them — too heavy.

She brought them out into the room and put them side by side on her mother's bed. Her breath caught in her throat when she opened them.

Dozens and dozens of boxes, all tied with bright red ribbon, the gift tags written out in her mother's careful script. Gayly colored Christmas stickers, sprigs of holly.

To Minta from Mother and Dad . . . to Grace from Mary . . . to John from Mary . . . to the Kelly Gremlins from Aunt Mary . . . to Uncle Art from the Hawley family . . .

"So you knew," Minta whispered the word. "You knew all the time."

. She looked down in surprise as a hot tear dropped on her hand and she dashed it away almost impatiently.

She picked up another package and read the tag. To Minta from Mother . . . with love.

She put all the other packages back in the suitcases and carried the cases back into the closet.

Poor Dad, she thought.

"She never knew," she could hear him saying. "Not even at the last."

Minta opened the box beside the bed and took out a sweater and pale green slip.

She brushed the tears away and went down the stairs and out into the cheerless living room.

"I'd like to keep these things, Dad," she said in her most matter-of-fact voice, and she showed him the sweater and slip. "The slip is a little big but I'll grow into it. It . . . it looks like her, I think."

She went around the room, snapping on the lamps, turning on the television that had been silent for so long. She was aware that his eyes followed her, that he could hardly avoid noticing the tear stains on her cheeks.

"I think I'll have an apple," she said. "Want one?"

He nodded. "Sure. Bring me one as long as you're making the trip."

It was natural. It was almost like old times, except that the blue chair by the fireplace was vacant.

She went out into the kitchen hurriedly.

"I'll tell him that I pestered Mother to do her shopping early this year," she told herself as she got the apples from the refrigerator. "I'll tell him that it was my idea. She wanted him to believe that she didn't know."

The vitamin pills were pushed back on a shelf. She took them out of the refrigerator and put them on the window sill where she would be sure to see them in the morning.

When she came back into the living room she noticed that a light in a Christmas wreath was winking on and off in the Kellys' window across the street.

"I guess we should start thinking about Christmas, Dad." She tossed him an apple as she spoke and he caught it deftly.

She hesitated for just a moment and then walked over and sat down in the blue chair by the fire, as if she belonged there, and looked across at her father, and smiled.

The Bell-Ringers

Sam Roddan

**It was as if someone had pulled a black bag
over my head so that I couldn't breathe.**

The church belfry was a wonderful place in the summer and I
don't think I have ever been so happy as on those cool Sunday
mornings when, after ringing the bell, Benny and I climbed up the
shaky ladder, wiggled through the trap door, and then, lying down on
the flat roof and peeking over the edge, watched the people hurrying
along the gravel paths in the Park by the mountain-ash trees.

"You know," Benny would say, "if we slept in one Sunday morning
and didn't ring the old bell, I bet nobody would come at all."

Rosedale was a sleepy little town with four churches, but the Baptist
was the only one with a bell besides ours. The manse where I lived was
right behind the church which was very handy because if it was raining
on a Sunday morning I could skip into the church without getting wet,
but Benny had to pedal his bike uphill all the way from the docks. But
even in the winter when the snow swirled across the lake, Benny was
never late. During the week days after school Benny would come over
to my place and we would stroll around the church, reading what the
sign at the front said about Pop's sermons for next Sunday, and
the time of the services, and when the church was built — which was
1905 — and then we made her snappy through the basement door up to
the kitchen where they served the hot bean suppers for the Tuxis Boys
on Friday nights, then to the back of the auditorium and up the stairs
to the bell room where the ropes were and the ladder for the trap door
to the belfry.

There were two ropes in the bell room. The big, heavy rope with the knot in it hung through a hole in the centre of the ceiling and was fastened to the wheel on the bell. Near the little round window that looked down on the street was the rope for the funerals. This rope was fixed to a big piece of iron which Benny called the "clapper", and when you pulled, it lifted the clapper which would then strike the bell and make a very deep and mournful sound. The big rope with the knot, which Benny and I pulled every Sunday at ten-thirty to get the people out for the service, moved the whole bell, and once you got her ringing you hung on to the rope and went up and down on it. After you had the knack, sometimes your head would nearly touch the ceiling. The bell was so strong and powerful it could take Benny and me both up the rope as though we were nothing. The ride was one of the reasons we were really crazy about the bell; that, and the sound, and the belfry from where we watched the town and everybody coming to church. Up in the belfry we were in a little world of our own, with only the bell, the sun, and the pigeons.

The pigeons at times got on our nerves. "I wouldn't mind one or two," Benny said, "because we could train them. But not this many. Look at the old bell, after we just polished her up yesterday."

Benny and I only went up into the belfry in the summer. It was too cold in the winter, and besides Benny had warned me that if it was thirty below and I touched the bell with my tongue, I would never get it off.

"The only way it could be done," Benny said, "would be to warm up the bell with a blow torch, and that's pretty dangerous because it would take out her temper and then we'd only have a rattle like the Baptist bell."

Neither Benny nor I liked pulling the funeral bell. There was no ride and besides a lot of people always seemed to be buried on Saturday afternoons when we had made plans to go to Three Mile Creek after Benny had finished helping Mr. McGuffey, the milkman, do his route. If it was somebody important and the funeral was during the week we would get notes from Pop to please excuse us from school. The services were usually at three and we got out half an hour earlier than the others. But if it was a long service, Benny and I had to stay in the bell room, and through the window we could see the other kids on the street with their books under their arms, watching for the coffin. As soon as Benny spotted Mr. Boom, the undertaker, walking solemnly down the church steps, he gave me the signal and I grabbed the funeral rope. Benny always wanted to give the signals until one day I saw he was waving at the kids. After that I felt we should take turns at giving signals, and Benny finally agreed. His point was that he didn't have to wear glasses and I did and he could see Mr. Boom better. But I could see from a distance pretty good too. Mr. Boom was a fat man with thick cheeks who always smoked big cigars except when he was on business. Some people said he slipped the silver handles off the coffins after everybody had gone home, but it was hard to say.

Benny was full of suggestions about looking after the bell. It was his idea to grease the bearings every day; to dry off the rope when it rained; and to keep track of the funerals. The idea here was that in the big beam that ran under the belfry roof we should make a notch each time we rang the funeral bell — a big notch if it was an important service, and a small notch if it was just an ordinary one. We kept the notches for about three months and then one day when we were up in the belfry looking around the old bell as usual, and examining the rope, and greasing her up a little, I asked Benny who the second notch from the end of the beam was, near the grease cup. Benny came over and said that was Mrs. Arbuckle. But then I started to think, if that was Mrs. Arbuckle, who was the notch on the other side of the grease cup? Benny said right away that was Mr. Johnson who used to run the hardware store. Well, I had him there, because Mr. Johnson was buried from the Baptist Church. After that we decided what's the use, and besides, as Benny pointed out, too many notches were weakening the beam; so we took some putty and filled them in and later whitewashed everything all over until it was as good as new.

Many wonderful things happened to Benny and me that summer, and while I'm trying hard to remember them all, it's just the big ones I'm telling about first. Sometimes on Saturday nights after dark we sneaked into the belfry and lay down on the flat roof beside the bell and looked at the town and listened to its mysterious noises. And, if there were boxing-matches in the Armouries across the street, from the belfry we had the best seats of all.

One night Mike Malinowski, who was the most famous boxer our town ever had, was fighting a big man from Toronto in black trunks, and Mike was getting knocked down on the mat then getting up and falling down again. And Mr. Boom was in the front row because we could see his fat cigar and his gold-plated watch chain and his little pigeon-eyes all bloodshot and mean. "He's waiting for Mike to kill the other guy," Benny said softly, not meaning it that way, because we couldn't believe anybody could ever knock Mike up and down like that. At the end, though, they lifted up Mike's hand, the way it should be because of a foul, while three men, including Mr. McGuffey, the milkman that Benny helped on Saturday mornings, held the Toronto fighter in his corner until they brought the police wagon and took him away.

"Someday I'll be a great boxer too," Benny said as we climbed back through the trap door that night, "and when I'm champ I'll let you wear my belt with all the diamonds in it."

It was the third week of August on a Saturday morning about nine o'clock when I heard the phone ring. I was just waking up and going over the plans for the day after Benny got back from helping Mr. McGuffey with his milk route. I was wondering whether we should try the different brand of grease on the bell that Benny had been discussing with Mr. Jackson, the garageman, when my mother cried out as though she had been hurt; then the phone receiver banged on the floor and I immediately figured it was broken for sure. Pop's voice started talking and said something about God's will, Mrs. McIvor, and God Moves in a Mysterious Way His Wonders to Perform; and then I really woke up, because I knew what it was. Benny's father had been sick for a long time and I would have to get right over to see Benny.

I pulled on my clothes, not figuring to wear my running-shoes because today would be different now, and black shoes were a mark of respect, and I went downstairs and asked Pop, who was staring into the receiver with his arm around mother, "When did it happen?"

Pop's voice sounded hollow, like the echoes you get from a mountain, and it was telling me that Benny had been out helping Mr. McGuffey, the milkman, and the horse had bolted off the dock.

I knew everything right then, the way you really know, and it was as if someone had pulled a black bag over my head so that I couldn't breathe. I sat down, staring at my shiny black shoes, and then I got up and took the receiver from Pop and checked to make sure it wasn't broken when it fell, and then I puttered around the kitchen for a while, half-figuring that the fishing was off for the day anyway, but not really thinking, trying to whistle a little bit even, and biting my lip, and not believing anything and knowing that everything was really over, so I went out and got on my bike and pedalled down to the dock, but all the way I could hardly breathe for the black bag, which wasn't there of course but which was keeping me from breathing.

There was a great crowd at the dock and a diver whose name I have forgotten was going down into the water. I watched Mr. Jackson, the garageman, working the air pumps, and waiting for a turn was Mr. McGuffey, who was sitting on an apple box with his head buried in his hands; and then I squirmed to the front where Mr. Jacobs, the school principal, was standing. Mr. Boom was already there, and so was Dr. Seldon. The bubbles were boiling up from the water coming from the air valves in the diver's suit, but when I got down on my hands and knees I could see the diver, half-floating like a big black fish on the bottom. He seemed to be dancing, and then I remembered what Benny said once about divers—that they have to wear leaden shoes on their feet for otherwise they would dance all over the bottom of the lake. I could see the wagon pretty clear but the name was too blurry to read.

Then I saw the horse. The diver was trying to bend over and undo the harness, but finally he had to crawl flat on his stomach and then he started to come up lifting the horse with one hand to the top of the water where Mr. Boom was ready with a rope which he slipped through the collar and made fast with a number eight knot on the cleat. Now the diver was going down again, moving his hands as though he were a huge black moth, and he balanced on the side of the wagon and pulled on the door. It came open pretty slowly and then I saw Benny swimming around inside. Benny was a very good swimmer and he looked as if he were coasting underwater at the Current River Pool, only here he had all his clothes on, which made the difference.

The diver moved like a very stupid moth with his big feet going up and down as though he were riding a bicycle, while Benny looked like a long sleek trout that knows exactly what he is doing because he slipped right out of the door, twisting in a graceful circle that I had never seen any swimmer do before. The diver didn't even know the first thing about swimming underwater. He could lift a horse with one hand to the top of the water but he couldn't catch Benny. Then the diver went into a little crouch with his big feet going up and down and I saw him clearly now with a long silver hook in his hand, and I knew that Benny didn't have a chance. Suddenly the water started to boil with white bubbles and the diver came to the surface with a great splash, and when the water had drained away Benny was resting over the diver's shoulders and Mr. Boom reached down, grabbed Benny by his collar, and flopped him on the dock.

I pedalled home very slowly and put away my bike figuring I wouldn't be needing it now, and in the garden I picked a few red raspberries but they were actually black currants I was eating and I have never been able to eat black currants, so I spat them out, and then I asked Mother where the red raspberries were. She told me they were over against the fence, at the back, beside the chicken coop where they have always been since I could remember. I ate a few red raspberries and tried the black currants again and went into the house biting my lip because the black currants were very bitter.

I guess it was on a Tuesday the funeral service was held. Anyway, everybody from the school was out, but before this, there had been a lot of talk about the pall-bearers. Pop thought it would be much better if the men teachers acted as pall-bearers, because you would not want the service interrupted by children who might stumble with the coffin. I figured that if we could carry big armfuls of wood into the basement, six fellows like Jim Brown and Stu Roberts and myself, who all played on the rugby team, could handle it easy. I had the argument, too, about the weights, because I had Benny's ticket on me from the weighing machine outside Mr. McCurdy's drug store. On Wednesday I had loaned Benny a penny to get weighed. And after he had read the ticket which said, "Still Waters Run Deep", he gave it to me because it was mine. But when he got his pay from Mr. McGuffey on Saturday I would give it back. We both weighed the same which was eighty-six pounds. But the real point, as I tried to explain to Pop, was that we were all volunteers. Anyway, the way it worked out, they made Jim and Stu and the other fellows ushers, and I guess it was all right. I was to look after the bell as usual, and things would be in the best interests of everyone concerned, was the way Pop finally explained it to us.

It was a big funeral because the people started coming about two o'clock to parade by the coffin and the service wasn't due until three. All the school kids were lined up to march past at two-thirty, and I got behind Jim Brown, who is a pretty good pal of mine, and we walked down the aisle and then past the flowers including the school wreath which was on the bottom part of the coffin. Benny had a little smile on his face and he seemed fine. I didn't look at him too long because there was an awful crush behind Jim and me, but I checked the silver handles and the inside lining which was smooth silk speckled with grey dots. It was the neatest coffin I have ever seen.

After Pop's sermon and before the last hymn, which was "Onward Christian Soldiers", I slipped out and went up to the bell room. Jim Brown, my pal, was to give me the high-sign from the street as soon as Mr. Boom came out the church door. I would then give the usual twelve strokes. At least that was the first idea. Then Jim and I figured, because we had been talking about this before the service, that for Benny we should give him eighteen—because he was nine, and twice nine is eighteen. So I agreed, although I knew I might have to speed up on the extra six to get down into Jim's father's car for the ride to the cemetery.

The bell room seemed a little empty without Benny but I was kept busy watching out the window, checking over the rope and waiting for Jim to give me the signal. As soon as Jim spotted Mr. Boom coming down the steps, he was to lift his right hand and point his finger to the sky, and then he would bow his head as a mark of respect to the dead. As I watched from the window I saw Jim take up his position on the sidewalk, and then his right arm started to go up and it seemed to me it was as high as it could go and I think he must have been on tip-toe although he never said later. Then he slowly bowed his head. Just as his head went down, so that of course he could only see his shoes, I saw Mr. Boom hurrying down the steps towards Jim, who was standing where he had to be to give me the signals. And Mr. Boom came up behind Jim and grabbed him by the collar and pushed him off the sidewalk onto the grass.

I can't quite tell how I felt then, but it was as if the silver handles were already in Mr. Boom's back pockets and he had a big fat cigar in his mouth and was spitting a great wallop of spit on the street. And so, because I didn't have much time left, yet making up my mind quickly because I could feel someone pulling a black bag over my head and not being able to breathe again, I reached over and grabbed the rope for the big bell.

And I let her have it. Gentle but firm at first, the way you have to be to get her swinging, but when the clang came at last it was like a clap of thunder. Then I leaned into the rope and feeling her burn into my hands I gave it everything I had. On the third swing I let the rope pile around my feet on the floor, then rode her right to the ceiling and pulled a double clang at the very peak, which Benny had always claimed was impossible. Then I got her going faster and faster and made another double clang and a triple rocket which was a special pull Benny had invented.

And now I rang the bell for all the glorious memories that were past and gone; for the great fishing expeditions; for the green grass down by Three Mile Creek; for the sweet smell of the mornings we tramped to Current River; for the long hours spent in the belfry planning great adventures; for the belt of sparkling diamonds that one day would have been Benny's; for all the quiet evenings when in silence we had watched our little town grown dim in the fading light. And I rang the bell for Benny's father and mother and for his sister, and Mr. McGuffey, and for my own aching heart.

It was on the last great pull and I was coasting to the ceiling for the triple rocket when I looked down and in the room I saw Mr. Boom and behind him was Jim, staring up at me. From the ceiling I saw their white faces and Mr. Boom's face was wide open and great tears were running down the creases into his mouth. And somehow at that moment I knew everything would be all right now, and so on the next time to the floor I let the rope burn out of my hands and we all stood together and watched it go up and down by itself until finally the old bell rolled to a halt and only the knot swished back and forth like a pendulum.

I put my hands in my pockets and Mr. Boom stepped back from the door and we went slowly down the steps. And outside in the bright sun all the people of the town were standing as far back as the mountain-ash trees in the Park, and they bowed their heads as a mark of respect to the dead and Mr. Boom led us to the chief mourners' car, which was crowded already with Benny's sister, Mr. and Mrs. McIvor, and Mr. McGuffey—but Mr. Boom squeezed Jim and me in and shut the door. And Benny's mother stared at my bleeding hands and I couldn't hear the torrent of words that spilled from her lips but my eyes were cool and very still, and I was not remembering much nor feeling hardly anything except knowing in my heart that we only do what we must when we pay respect to the memories of a great man.

The Elk Tooth Dress

Dorothy M. Johnson

She dug in the big bag she carried and
brought out something. It was her little old
short cape embroidered with porcupine quills,
dyed in soft colors long ago. She hung it over
my shoulders, and I felt warm and cared
for. . . .

Joe Red Crane came over to talk about us going to the Indian
Institute in Missoula. It is a big gathering at the University with
meetings for several days, to talk about the problems of Indians, and
have we got problems! Grandpa said that this year he would let the
professors talk about the problems and he would just as soon be in the
big show in the University Field House after they got the problems all
talked about.

Sometime, maybe, I will learn how to get around Grandma, but
Grandpa still can't do it, and he has been married to her for thirty-five
years. I am only sixteen years old. They are both old-fashioned, but
Grandpa is not so stubborn.

Grandpa wanted to wear his own grandfather's feather war bonnet
in the big show, but Joe Red Crane talked him out of it. That shows
the difference between Grandpa and Grandma. Nobody ever talked
her out of anything.

"This old war bonnet is the real thing," Grandpa argued in the
Salish language. "The feathers are broken because it is old and been
kicked around."

"It don't look like much," Mr. Red Crane said. "Now we want to look real good, don't we? You know how these Blackfeet dress up all fancy. They are stylish dancers, too. You want us Flatheads to put on a good show, don't you?"

Grandpa snorted and said in English, "Good show? Our folks used to lick the daylights out of them Blackfeet when we went hunting buffalo on the east side of the mountains. Blackfeet! Humph!"

"But you weren't there," Mr. Red Crane said.

Grandpa yelped. "Hey, what tribe you belong to, Joe? You Blackfeet now, Joe?"

"Now, now," said Mr. Red Crane. "I'm Flathead, like you."

"You are no Flathead," said Grandpa. "You are some kind of mail-order Indian. Where did you get that feather outfit you wore at the Arlee Pow-Wow? Sent away for it some place, that's what you did. And what about them tail feathers you got? Our people didn't wear tail feathers in the old days. I wouldn't be caught dead in tail feathers."

He switched back to Salish again. "I am not going to dance in Missoula," he said, and started to put the broken old war bonnet back in its box.

Mr. Red Crane got worried, but he knows how to get around Grandpa, who is old-fashioned.

"We better smoke about this," he said.

So Grandpa got out his old, long pipe and they sat on the floor in the parlour. Grandma didn't even say anything about ashes on her nice clean floor, because she likes old-fashioned ways.

After a while, Mr. Red Crane said, "You are the best dancer on the Flathead Reservation."

"There is no doubt about that," answered Grandpa.

"You got real style," Mr. Red Crane said.

"I sure have," said Grandpa.

"You don't even have to wear bells on your ankles when you dance. You don't have to dress up or anything. You get a tremendous hand just because you dance so good."

"That is absolutely right," said Grandpa.

"So you will dance at the Indian Institute in Missoula, maybe?"

"Now you put it that way, maybe I will," said Grandpa. "But I won't wear tail feathers or no mail-order war bonnet. I will just wear my beaded vest."

"You will also wear pants," Grandma said to him over her shoulder.

Grandpa said, "All the time I meant to wear pants. Women should stay out of serious conversations."

"There would be serious conversations if you went to Missoula with no pants," Grandma answered.

Then Mr. Red Crane got around to noticing me. I was doing my homework, and you can bet it is hard to memorize irregular French verbs when you are listening to a conversation that switches from English to Salish and back.

"We got to have a nice display of art work for the exhibit," he said. "You going to bring something pretty, Natalie? I bet you are. Some nice beadwork."

"I don't like beadwork," I said. "It's old-fashioned. I don't think I will go anyway. Not unless I can get my hair cut short and have a permanent."

Grandma said to the wall, "Natalie will go, and she will not have a permanent. She will wear her hair in braids like she was meant to. She has not got her exhibit finished yet, but she will. It is a bag all covered with beads." Grandma switched to Salish and muttered, "She is lazy. Bad girl."

I am only kind of lazy and not very bad, but I did not argue, because getting a permanent is something we have not agreed about for two years or more.

Joe Red Crane saved his talk with Grandma till last, because it was going to be the toughest.

"And you will wear your fringed buckskin dress with the elk teeth all over it," he said to her with a big smile," and you will be in the Grass Dance."

"I will not do any such thing," said Grandma. "I am going to wear my go-to-town clothes and sit in the audience and watch everybody and see whether my old man is wearing his pants. Natalie can wear my dress with the elk teeth if she wants to. I guess she won't want to, though, because she has all these modern ideas."

I almost jumped out of my chair. She had never let me wear that dress before. It is very old and valuable. If I asked her for it, she would have said, "No, you are careless, you would lose some of the elk teeth."

"That's all settled then," Mr. Red Crane said, getting up off the floor.

After he left, I went to work on Grandma, figuring that if I said no, she would say yes.

"I don't want to get my braids cut off and have a permanent," I said. "I have decided to wear my hair long even if you do have to work so hard brushing it."

"Good thing," she said, "because that is how it is going to be."

At school all the kids were talking about going to Missoula, and when I found out some more about the plans, I got pouty.

"I am not going to go," I told Grandma. "Mary MacTavish is going to be introduced as a princess because her great-grandfather was a chief and signed some old treaty. She would have flunked algebra if I had not helped with her homework. So now she is a princess. Mary MacTavish — some Indian!"

Grandma got a wicked look on her face and said, "The Scottish fur traders were very busy around here in the old days, but not in my family or your grandfather's. Just be proud you're a full-blood and never mind the princess stuff. But you will go."

Now I am glad I went, because it was a lovely time. It was the most wonderful time I can remember.

That was a big affair, that Indian Institute at the University Field House in Missoula. Grandpa even washed the station wagon. He spent so much time on it that Grandma got nervous and said she would rather ride in a car with mud on it than get there after everybody else left. But we got there early.

We had the biggest bunch of people from our reservation because we only had to go a few miles. There were people from tribes all over Montana, strangers, handsome people in beautiful costumes. Second to us, the Blackfeet had the biggest bunch and Grandma said, "Huh! The women wear rouge."

There were more languages being spoken than I had ever heard before — Indian languages, all different. Absolutely nobody said one word in French. Sometimes, I wonder why I go to all the trouble with those irregular verbs. One good thing about Salish, nobody fusses about grammar. You just talk it.

It was a wonderful time, the gathering of all those dark, dignified people — my people, even if they were from other tribes with other languages. The whites came too, of course, lots of them, but they were just there to see us.

In the big crowd we lost track of Grandpa.

"Now where is that Indian exhibit?" Grandma muttered, and I said,

"I don't want to go see that."

"I should think you wouldn't," she answered, "but we are going to see it anyway."

It was embarrassing because I never did finish my beadwork exhibit and Grandma had to. She fussed because she had to do it kind of sloppy so nobody would know it wasn't all mine. But after all, when a girl is a junior in high school and studying French, and she's in a lot of activities, how much time has she got for beadwork?

We found the exhibit. Grandma asked an Indian where it was. She wouldn't ask a white person because she wouldn't admit they might know something she didn't.

Mary MacTavish was hanging around the exhibit, because her entry for art work was a drawing of Marilyn Monroe that she copied out of a movie magazine. Mary MacTavish, that princess, stood around in her mail-order buckskin dress batting her eyelashes, and I must admit she had two fellows from our football team and two others hanging around with her.

"Oh, hello, Natalie," she said very sweetly, for fear I wouldn't notice all those fellows, and I said, "Hiya, princess, old kid."

Grandma said in a carrying voice, "We will not look at any drawings copied out of magazines. We will look at the real Indian art. Well, that bag you beaded looks pretty good, Natalie. They displayed it nice."

I kind of nudged my arm against her arm to tell her I was grateful that she didn't give away my guilty secret about not finishing it myself, and she nudged back. When Grandma is for you, she is for you all the way especially if somebody else is against you.

"Where did that old man of mine go?" she grumbled.

"He just came in," I said, "with a white woman," and Grandma said, "What!"

Grandpa was being very Noble Red Man. He is not very tall, but he can look awful noble. He was just looking past this white woman in a baggy tweed suit and not answering her, and she was getting more and more earnest, pointing at her camera and talking her idea of Indian English. "Me take picture, okay? You stand still, me take nice picture?"

I was so grateful to Grandma for being on my side that I walked over and rescued him for her, because she wouldn't lower herself by chasing after him.

I said to him in Salish, "Come on with me if you want to get away."

The white woman said, "Little girl, maybe you talk English — just tell him I want to take his picture."

So if she wanted to, why didn't she go ahead?

I murmured, *"Je ne parle pas l'anglais. Mon grandpere ne parle pas l'anglais."*

She shook her head and said, "Oh, dear. They all talk Indian," and walked away.

Then we three went to the Field House and got settled in the front row of the audience.

We looked around and I saw the most beautiful thing I ever laid eyes on. He was tall and lean, in blue jeans and cowboy boots, and he had long hair. Long, thick, glossy braids, even if he was young like me — long hair like the old men, but ah, how pretty it looks on a young fellow!

He was as handsome as a calendar, with a sharp profile and his head held high. He wore a cowboy hat, sort of tipped back so it wouldn't hide the soft way his hair came down over his ears, because he was proud of his hair, and that was right.

Alongside him, all the boys I know look just plain stupid. My heart hurt, I kind of wanted to cry.

I said in a whisper, "Grandma, look."

"Look at what?" she asked. "All those strange Indians?"

Then I saw he was not by himself but in a group of five or six men, all older, but do you know, I hadn't noticed them before. They were Indians but wearing business suits, and a couple of them had braids.

Grandma saw the young man then and said, "Ah." She said something to Grandpa and he looked and said, "Ah."

Then he got up and ambled over to these men halfway across the arena and they all got acquainted and shook hands. The young long-hair didn't talk; he just stood there listening, the way a young man should in the presence of his betters only generally they don't.

Grandma said, "They are Cheyennes," and I asked, "How can you tell from here?"

"Your grandpa just told me in sign talk," she answered. "If you'd keep your eyes open, you might learn something. The young fellow is going to be in the show." She squinted and added, "His name is something like water."

It just goes to show you how much good French does a girl when something really important comes up. I don't pay much attention to sign talk, it's old-fashioned. We used to use it in grade school when we wanted to make remarks about a new teacher.

"Oh, look at that mail-order princess," I said, shocked. "She is going right over to interrupt the men. She is going to get that Cheyenne boy for herself."

"I don't think she is," said Grandma. "Keep still and trust your grandpa. Sometimes he is a no-good, but in a pinch you can depend on him."

Mary was heading for the men, with two other girls, all giggling and wiggling. But Grandpa fixed her wagon. It was cute how he did it. He never glanced around, never saw those fresh girls right behind him, trying to attract his attention, trying to interrupt. He never saw them, but every time Mary moved a little to one side, he moved too, so his back was always toward her while he talked to the other men.

There was quite a crowd of Indians around there, making a quiet fuss over the long-hair boy. The old people approved because he was conservative, old-fashioned, and the boys hung around because he was twirling a rope, sort of playing with it, and the girls edged up because he was so cute. And I had to stay by Grandma because we are conservative.

Grandma said, "Never mind that phony Minnehaha, making eyes. You make eyes at the ground. . . Listen, I saw some other women from other reservations with elk teeth on their dresses, but not so many as on the dress you're wearing. Don't you worry."

She dug in the big bag she carried and brought out something. It was her little old short cape embroidered with porcupine quills, dyed in soft colors long ago. She hung it over my shoulders, and I felt warm and cared for because I knew she thought a lot of me and was on my side.

Even when she was a child, not many women were embroidering with porcupine quills; they used all beads because it was easier. This cape was very old, made by her grandmother. The buckskin was soft and gray, not dirty but not glaring white. Wearing it, I felt like a queen and was not very jealous of Princess MacTavish.

The men and boys from our reservation were buckling on the bells they wear on their legs for dancing, and you couldn't hear yourself think. They are big round bells with something noisy inside. And Grandpa had gone over to the middle and started beating a drum.

The only thing he doesn't like about a show is that he can't beat a drum and dance at the same time.

Then a man said, "Woof, woof, testing," into the public address system, and asked everybody to take his seat because the show was going to begin. The young long-hair walked past us with his friends but he did not look our way at all.

Grandma said, "Natalie, stop looking at him all the time."

"What does he wear long hair for if he doesn't want to be looked at?" I answered.

"I don't know what he wants," said Grandma, "but I want you to stop looking. He will think you are bold."

"He doesn't know I'm alive," I moaned, and she said with a satisfied chuckle, "Oh yes, he does. What do you think your grandpa went over there for? To talk about the hay crop, maybe?"

I was so happy I even stopped staring.

Grandma said, "Doesn't Mary MacTavish look silly with her short hair in that Indian dress from mail order? But you look just right."

"I am a bad girl and lazy," I said. "You had to finish my beadwork."

"Oh, not so bad," she answered, always arguing.

Somebody on the public address system made a long speech about the significance of all this and named all the tribes that were represented, and then he said the Flatheads would please take their places. So I left Grandma and went drifting out to the arena with the rest of our people and stood with the other girls in the back.

The men sat down in chairs in a long row. The chairs were turned backward because if a man wears tail feathers he has to straddle when he sits down. But Grandpa turned his chair around and leaned back and was comfortable, because he wouldn't be caught dead in those mail-order tail feathers. He had a big silver ornament on each braid, but he wasn't dressed up except for a beaded vest. He wore his pants all right, blue jeans. He wore his silver-rimmed glasses, too, and Grandma didn't like that; she says it is too modern. But he says, "I am nearsighted and I wear glasses. You want me to fall over something and break my neck, maybe?"

Mary MacTavish said to me, "Hi, kid. It's too bad they won't let me present you to the audience. Alice and Elizabeth are my maids-in-waiting, you know. I am going to present them to the audience. But I can't do a thing for you, because their ancestors signed the same treaty mine did, but your ancestors wouldn't sign."

"My ancestors never gave the country away," I said. "They wanted to hang onto it."

"What you looking at the ground for?" she asked. "Lost something?"

"Indian girls are supposed to be modest," I said. "Didn't anybody ever tell you? I am a full-blood, so I am going to be modest while I've got this elk tooth dress on and this old and valuable embroidered cape all covered with dyed porcupine quills."

"I guess you're just jealous because I'm not going to present you too," Mary MacTavish said.

"I guess you better be kind of polite," I said, "if you don't want to flunk French."

Then we had to quit talking, because Mr. Red Crane started to talk on the PA system, introducing our people.

There were a couple of dances for the men, good and noisy, with all the drumming and all those bells on their legs clanging with every step, and I was in the Grass Dance with Mary and the rest of them.

Mr. Red Crane introduced Princess Mary MacTavish, and she walked forward with her beaded moccasins on her feet and her permanent on her head, looking so modest it would kill you, making eyes at the ground.

"Princess Mary will now present her maids-in-waiting," Mr. Red Crane said, and everybody waited, but she didn't. She was being so modest, she just stood there. So Alice had to walk out by herself, and so did Elizabeth.

Then *they* just stood there, the modest Indian maidens, until the announcer told them twice they could go sit down now.

Then he said, "One of the girls from the Flathead Reservation is wearing a very rare costume, very old, that I am sure you will want to see. Natalie Root Digger, will you please walk forward so the audience can see you?"

Well, I just about died, I only went forward about three steps and stood there with my eyes down, feeling those thousands of people staring. He told about the old dress with the elk teeth on it and the precious cape with the porcupine-quill embroidery and the people clapped. I went back without anybody telling me.

I never took my eyes off the ground, but I saw that long-hair Cheyenne in the front row sitting by Grandma. She looked good. She wore her black dress with red figures in it, and her best purple silk handkerchief draped around her head in folds, with her long dark braids looped to hang down under it.

Later, they did more dances, and Grandpa would sneak out in front of the rest and kind of clown with his dancing. Every time he did that, the audience would laugh and clap. Then we went out of the arena and finally I got over to where Grandma was. She said in Salish, "Sit down. Lots of room," and the long-hair started to get up out of the way. But Grandma said in English, "Stay there. She's little, she won't crowd you."

He said, "She sure won't," and we sat close because we had to, both looking at the ground but seeing each other just the same.

He had the most wonderful voice, deep and soft and bashful.

The announcer said now the Blackfeet would come in and perform, and Grandma said, "Huh!"

All the other Indians, when they had gone into the arena, had just sort of drifted in. But those Blackfeet came marching to a drum, very showy, and their leader gave them signals with an eagle wing fan. Real fancy.

The long-hair boy said, "Tourist stuff," and Grandma looked at him with approval.

They did some dances and they were so popular with the silly crowd of white people that they kept right on doing dances. The Cheyenne boy made a thoughtful sound and got up and walked across the arena toward Grandpa and the rest of our Flathead men. In a minute, Grandpa and the others from our reservation started walking from one end of the arena toward the other.

You should have heard it. They didn't do anything but just walk and mind their own business, but when two dozen Indians walk from one place to another with strings of big bells on their legs, not keeping step — well. The racket was so loud, with the clanging of the bells drowning out the Blackfeet drums, that the audience forgot about the Blackfeet dancing, so smart and sassy. People got kind of fidgety and started looking at their programs and when they clapped for the Blackfeet, Grandma and I clapped for the Flatheads.

Grandma said, "Well, I guess we won *that* battle."

When the young long-hair came back, drifting, Grandma moved over so he would sit between us.

"What's your name, Cheyenne?" she asked.

"George Standing in the Water," he answered.

"You're a smart boy," Grandma said, "and I would like to meet your folks sometime."

He didn't say anything, but he blushed. A blush under a bronze skin is pretty.

"Your folks are old-fashioned?" Grandma asked him, and he knew it was a compliment and nodded.

"My brother fasted in the Sun Dance last year," he said. "Maybe I will some day."

We don't do the Sun Dance — we have our own customs — but I knew a little about that, and I shivered. They starve and don't drink any water, the few men who dare to dance the Sun Dance, for four days; then they dance until they faint sometimes.

"Maybe we'll come to your reservation sometime," Grandma purred.

"I wouldn't want to see the Sun Dance if anybody I knew was in it," I said, feeling terrible.

"My brother's girl, she was kind of proud of him," George said. So then I thought I could watch him if the time came, and I would be proud too.

The announcer said on the PA system, "A young Cheyenne from the Tongue River Reservation will demonstrate his skill in roping. I present George Standing in the Water, of the Northern Cheyennes."

George went out in the arena, not very far, not looking up at the audience, but as if he was there all by himself with nobody around. It was all quiet, no drumming. He twirled his rope in little circles and big circles. He danced into the spinning rope circle and danced out of it again. The rope was like a live thing that did just what he wanted it to do, and his hands hardly moved, but the rope spun its circle and rippled and flashed like water.

People were taking pictures—flash, flash went the cameras, taking pictures of the fine long-hair. Grandpa's white-woman girl friend was jumping around in her baggy tweed suit, putting new flash bulbs in her camera and taking pictures and talking to herself.

It was as if George was there all alone, in the big Field House, dreaming with the spinning rope. When he stopped, there was nothing dramatic about the stopping. He didn't bow to the audience like some performers do. Why should he bow? He didn't owe them anything. He just gathered up his rope when he was through, while the audience clapped and hollered, and he walked over to sit by us again.

I thought, I wish I had a camera. I wish I could have a picture of George Standing in the Water to keep forever.

Somebody made another long speech about the significance of all this, and some other tribes danced, and then the whole show was over. Grandpa drifted over to us, and that white woman in the tweed suit made a dive at him.

"Well. I'll take care of *this*," said Grandma and marched toward them like an army with banners.

"You going home tonight?" George asked, looking at the ground.

I said, "Yes. To Arlee." And maybe I will never see you again, I thought. That will be worse than if I never had known you were alive. "Where you going?"

"Staying at a motel with my friends. Long drive to Tongue River. We'll start early in the morning. Listen, where would a fellow write you a letter if he wanted to, maybe? Just Arlee?"

"That's right. Natalie Root Digger, Arlee, Montana." Then I got really bold. "You know, we dig bitterroot around Missoula in the spring, pretty soon. We're old-fashioned. We don't mind if our friends come dig bitterroot with us. Or maybe you have to go to school."

"This year I have to go to school. I am on the track team. Maybe next year. If your folks come to our rodeo. I ride bucking horses."

"Maybe Grandma and Grandpa would like to go to your rodeo," I answered. "I guess they would probably take me along."

We never looked at each other all that time, but I saw his black, soft, shining braids, and he saw my braids, and the buckskin dress trimmed with elk teeth and the little cape with the faded-colour porcupine-quill embroidery.

"Well, so long," he said.

I said, "Okay. See you around."

He walked away, so lithe and slim, and my heart wanted to cry.

My folks came back, with their faces straight but I could tell they were laughing inside about something. I didn't feel like laughing.

"Well, that white woman got your grandpa's picture," Grandma said. "It's hard talking this Injun English she likes, but I got the idea across that she could take his picture if she would send me a print; also she has to send me some other pictures that are on the same roll of film."

"That's nice," I said with my heart jumping. Because she had taken pictures of George while he was spinning the rope.

"Where'd that Cheyenne go?" Grandma asked.

"He had to catch up with his friends. Grandma, he asked us to their rodeo and I asked him to help us dig bitterroot, and is it all right? If you say it's wrong and I'm not a nice modest girl, I'll just die!"

"It is all right and you are a good girl," she answered. "I think we will maybe go to the Cheyennes' rodeo when the time comes."

When my letter comes from the Tongue River Reservation, it will have his return address on it, I guess. But I wouldn't ask him for it, because it is a good thing to be old-fashioned, even for a girl who is a junior in high school and learning French.

Hurt

Alden Nowlan

When Stevie cried it was never for the reasons the rest of the kids cried.

"**W**hen I grow up there ain't nothin' ever gonna hurt me. Not ever," Stevie used to tell me, doubling up his grimy fists until his knuckles whitened, and snarling like a small, trapped animal, a fox or a feral cat maybe, as he squeezed back the tears at the corners of the eyes that looked ridiculously huge in his peaked ten-year-old's face.

He'd say that after the health nurse sent him home from school because there were lice in his whiskey-coloured mop of hair again or after one of the kids teased him about his old man getting drunk and losing his job at the mill for probably the tenth time that summer, and maybe after Mom or somebody tried to give him a second-hand polo shirt.

The only plans I'd made for growing up were that I was going to be a cowboy, a locomotive engineer, a pirate and maybe pitcher for the Brooklyn Dodgers. Stevie lived in a trailer across the bridge from our farm. I thought it must be wonderful to live in a trailer and not have somebody yelling at you all the time to take off your rubbers when you came in the house.

Stevie's old man yelled at him plenty but only when he was drunk. When he was sober he let him do whatever he liked. Stevie went to school when he wanted to go and when he was bored with it he stayed home or spent the day on the marsh or in the woods. He fixed his own meals and sometimes ate six chocolate bars and a bottle of pop for supper.

Stevie wasn't like any of the other kids who came to school in dirty sweat shirts and were sent home lousy. There were a dozen kids in

Hastings Mills public school like that. Muscular thirteen-year-olds spending their fifth year in Grade V, knowing that next year they'd be free to chuck their exercise books and get a job on somebody's farm or at the mill. Wet-nosed little girls who wore wrinkled dresses that almost tickled their ankles and stole everything from the Junior Red Cross treasury to the buttons on the teacher's coat. Stevie never studied and he was usually at the head of the class. When he wasn't in first place it was because he'd stayed home the week we had exams, lying on his belly in the grass in front of the trailer reading a book old man Simms had given him, or picking lady's slippers in the swamp or building the biggest kite we'd ever seen, or something like that. Old man Simms was supposed to be crazy and rich. Eventually he was buried by the parish. Every Hallowe'en he patrolled his farm with a shotgun loaded with rock salt. Naturally, stealing his mail box was the finest adventure of the year. He liked Stevie and gave him a book called *The Boy's Book of Heroes*, all about people like Xerxes and Xenophon and Achilles and Napoleon. Stevie read it all that summer we were ten. When I went over to the trailer after school or on Saturdays and suggested we play war, I always wanted to fight Nazis, but Stevie wouldn't play unless we fought Persians or Trojans.

The more Trojans we killed in the games the better Stevie like it. We picked cat-tails in the swamp, dried them in the sun and used them as torches when we razed Troy. Stevie sprinkled half a box of salt on the burnt grass and said that's what you were supposed to do when you conquered a city because then "there won't never be anything grow there any more." At the end I always had to be Hector and he was Achilles and killed me with a wooden sword. He swung the sword with furious intensity, forcing me to back away from him. His teeth clenched and his eyes were slits in his white face. He was quick as a cat and sometimes sharp smacks from the sword on my arms and chest goaded me into bringing my stave down on his shoulder or wrist with all my strength and anger behind the blow so that it left a red blotch that gradually turned blue wherever it hit. After hitting him I was always ashamed. But he'd say, "That's the way, Skip, that's the way to do it," and keep boring in until we agreed that I was dead and went swimming.

Stevie couldn't bear to see real things die. My brother Chuck let us go out with him to try out a new .22 and Stevie liked watching him shoot holes through a tomato can and knock chips off the fence posts but when he sent a squirrel spinning out of a tree and we walked over and looked down at the little limp bundle of fur and blood, Stevie's lips were shivering as if someone had dropped an icicle down the neck of his shirt and his eyes looked exactly like those of a fawn the dogs killed one winter in the field back of our house.

"Why did you have to kill it?" he said and Chuck looked down at him, not knowing what to say, and Stevie started crying, pressing his palms into his eyes.

The winter after that, he found all of Bill Taylor's rabbit snares and stole them.

Sometimes when I went over to the trailer, Stevie's old man was drunk on moonshine or homebrew or vanilla extract. One Saturday he'd be lying on the sofa with his shirt and boots off, singing at the top of his voice and ending each verse with an explosion of laughter. Then next Saturday he'd be pounding the walls with his fists and swearing and crying at the same time or maybe lying on the floor or in the grass, snoring and mumbling in his sleep, waking up every little while to vomit.

When he was happy-drunk and wanted to sing he gave Stevie cigarettes. When it was summer we sat on the ground behind the trailer, with our bare knees drawn up under our chins, and smoked, with Stevie inhaling like a man and me just letting the cigarette burn down as I held it in my mouth. Stevie had no "respect" for his old man, not the kind of respect Pop was always telling me I was supposed to have for him, but when he passed out and started shivering Stevie threw a coat over his shoulders. And Sunday mornings when the old man was too sick to go himself, Stevie went down to the store and got him a couple of bottles of vanilla to sober up on.

Sometimes I met him on my way to Sunday School, me itching and sweating in my starched shirt and my toes aching in leather shoes. He'd be barefoot and wearing a pair of dirty denim shorts. He'd have the vanilla bottles in a paper bag and maybe be carrying something crazy like a big bouquet of daisies in the other hand. Once or twice I went back to the trailer with him and after the old man drank the vanilla he'd give us whatever change he had in his pockets and we'd go back to the store and buy some chocolate bars with old Mason, the storekeeper, teasing me about what Pop would do to me if he found out about me running around with Stevie when I was supposed to be in Sunday School, and then short-changing us because he knew I wouldn't dare tell. Stevie wasn't afraid to tell, but he ignored it. He took it for granted that people were going to cheat him every chance they got.

Then we'd go swimming in the creek and I'd feel free and fine, pulling my torturing Sunday clothes off and feeling the soreness ooze out of my feet when we ran across the cool mud toward the water. One Sunday on the creek bank Stevie tried to teach me to play cards, giving me half his money and then manipulating the pieces of greasy pasteboard until he'd won it all back.

He didn't laugh when he won. Stevie seldom laughed at anything. When he smiled it wasn't a kid's grin. I thought it was like Mom smiled sometimes when you weren't quite sure she was smiling at you or at anything you could see but maybe at something inside her you couldn't understand, something that was even a little sad. Stevie found a duck with a broken leg and made it a splint out of a shingle and kept it in a box in the trailer, trying to get it to eat bread crumbs, and after a week it died. When he knelt down to coax it to eat he always had that funny, sad little smile.

When he did laugh his whole body vibrated with it and he'd roll on the ground, hugging himself and laughing, until tears ran down his cheeks and he blew his nose and rocked back and forth, trying to get his breath. His laughter always scared me a little and I'd punch him in the chest and yell at him and once I threw a dipperful of cold water in his face and he only laughed harder.

When Stevie cried it was never for the reasons the rest of the kids cried. Miss Grant, who taught school at Hastings Mills the year I was ten, strapped him every time he skipped school and while she was smacking him he bit his lower lip and blinked at the blackboard and after it was over he went back to his desk and spat on his palms and thumbed his nose at her elaborately as she turned her back, so that everyone laughed.

But one noon hour when he had nothing for lunch except a gooey chocolate bar and she offered him some of her sandwiches, he bolted away from her and afterwards I found him in the woodshed, lying face down in the sawdust, his shoulders shaking with sobs.

That was one of the times that he told me when he grew up nothing was ever going to hurt him.

"When I grow up, Skip, there ain't nothin' ever gonna hurt me," he said. But he didn't stop crying.

The Friday Everything Changed

Anne Hart

**Miss Ralston waited, her sturdy feet braced
against the cinders, her body rocking with the
bat.**

The last hour of school on Friday afternoons was for Junior Red
Cross. The little kids would get out their Junior Red Cross pins and
put them on, and us big kids would start elbowing down the aisles to
the book cupboard at the back to see who would get the interesting
magazines. There was a big pile of them and they were of two kinds:
the *National Geographic* and the *Junior Red Cross News*. Because the
boys were stronger and sat near the back they usually got the *National
Geographics* first, which meant they could spend the rest of Red Cross
looking at African ladies wearing nothing on top, while us girls had
to be satisfied with the *Junior Red Cross News*, which showed little
African kids wearing lots of clothes and learning how to read. Apart
from the magazines for the big kids and maybe the teacher reading a
story to the little kids, about the only other thing that happened
regularly during Red Cross was picking the two boys who would carry
water the next week.

In our school the water bucket always stood on a shelf at the front
of the room just behind the teacher's desk. First you'd make a paper
cup out of a piece of scribbler paper, then you'd grab the teacher's
attention from wherever it happened to be and then up you'd go to
the front of the room for a drink from the water bucket.

It was kind of interesting to stand at the front of the room behind
the teacher's desk and drink water. The school looked different from
up there and sometimes you could get just a glimpse of an idea of what
the teacher thought she was all about. I mean, from the front,

looking down on those rows of kids with their heads bent over their desks and the sun coming in the windows and the blackboards and all that stuff on the walls, you might almost think, at first glance, that you were looking at one of those real city schools—like in the health books — where the kids were all so neat and all the same size. But after that first strange moment it just became our old school again, because you had to start adding in things like the coal stove and the scarred old double desks and the kids themselves. I mean, we just didn't look like the kids in those pictures. Maybe it was because we were so many different sizes — from the little kids snuffling in the front rows over their Nan and Dan readers to the big boys hunched over their desks at the back—maybe it was because we wore so many heavy clothes all the time, or maybe it was because of something that wasn't even there at all but seemed to be on the faces of the kids in those city pictures: a look as if they liked being where they were.

But all that's a long way from Junior Red Cross and who would carry the water.

The water for our school came from a pump at the railway station, which was about a quarter of a mile away. One day long ago a health inspector had come around and had announced that water must be made available to the school. For a while there had even been some talk of digging a well but in the end we got a big, shiny, galvanized water bucket and permission to use the railway station pump. And from that day on—for all the boys—the most important thing that happened at school, even more important than softball, was who would get to carry the water.

If you were a boy it was something you started dreaming about in grade 1, even though there was not the remotest chance it could ever happen to you before at least grade 5, and only then if the teacher thought you were big and strong enough. You dreamed about it partly because carrying the water meant you were one of the big guys, and carrying the water meant you could get away from school for maybe half an hour at a time. But mostly you dreamed about it because carrying the water was something real, and had absolutely nothing whatever to do with Nan and Dan and all that stuff.

So every Friday afternoon toward the end of Red Cross, when it got to be time for the teacher to pick the two boys who would go for water the next week, all the National Geographics came to rest like huge butterflies folding up their yellow wings and a big hush fell all over the back rows. And that's the way it had always been until one extraordinary afternoon when, right out of the blue, just after the teacher had picked Ernie Chapman and Garnet Dixon to carry the water, my seatmate, Alma Niles, put up her hand and said: "Why can't girls go for the water, too?"

If one of those planes, like in the war movies, had suddenly appeared over the school and dropped a bomb, we all couldn't have been more surprised. A silence fell over the room and in the silence everyone looked at the teacher.

Now our teacher that year was named Miss Ralston and even though she came from River Hibbert we all liked her quite a lot. She was strict but she was never really mean like some of the teachers we'd had. Because she was young (she'd just finished grade 11 the year before herself — River Hibbert had fancy things like grade 11) she'd had quite a rough time the first week of school with the bigger boys. But she was pretty big herself and after she'd strapped most of them up at the front of the room before our very eyes (and even the little kids could see that it really hurt) things had settled down. The boys kind of admired Miss Ralston for strapping so hard, and us girls admired her because she was so pretty and wore nylon stockings and loafers all the time. But the really unusual thing about Miss Ralston was the way she sometimes stopped in the middle of a lesson and looked at us as if we were real people, instead of just a lot of kids who had to be pushed through to their next grades. And that was why, on that Friday afternoon when Alma Niles put up her hand and said: "Why can't girls go for the water, too?" we all turned and looked at Miss Ralston first instead of just bursting out laughing at Alma right away.

And Miss Ralston, instead of saying, "Whoever heard of girls going for the water?" or, "Are you trying to be saucy, Alma?" like any other teacher would, said nothing at all for a moment but just looked very hard at Alma, who had gone quite white with the shock of dropping such a bombshell. After a long moment, when she finally spoke, Miss Ralston, instead of saying, "Why that's out of the question, Alma," threw a bombshell of her own: "I'll think about that," she said—as if, you know, she *would* — "and I'll let you know next Friday."

The trouble started right away as soon as we got into the schoolyard, because all the boys knew, from the moment Miss Ralston had spoken, that something of theirs was being threatened and that, as long as there was the remotest chance that any girl might get to carry the water, they had to do everything in their power to stop it. Like driving a tractor or playing hockey for the Toronto Maple Leafs, carrying the water was real, and because it was real it belonged to them.

So they went right for Alma as soon as she came out of school and that was when another funny thing happened. Instead of just standing back and watching Alma get beaten up, as we usually did when the boys were after someone, the girls rushed right in to try and help her. In the first place we all liked Alma, and in the second place we all had seen, as clearly as the boys, what our carrying the water might mean: that, incredibly, we, too, might get to skip school for half an hour at a time, that we, too, might get to sneak into Rowsell's store on the way back and, most dizzying thought of all, that we too might get to do something real.

And, because we were so intoxicated by the whole idea, and took the boys so much by surprise by standing up to them, we somehow managed to get Alma and ourselves out of the schoolyard with only a few bruises and torn stockings, leaving the boys in possession of the schoolyard where, as we could glimpse over our shoulders as we ran down the hill, they had begun to gather together in a single ominous knot.

And for the rest of that weekend, though of course we never talked about it in front of our parents, all we could think of, both boys and girls, was what was going to happen at school that coming week.

The first thing, clearly evident by recess on Monday morning, was that the boys had decided not to let us girls field at softball any more.

Softball at our school used to go like this: every Monday morning at recess two of the bigger boys — that year it was usually Ernie Chapman and Junior LeBlanc — used to pick their teams for the week. Whoever came out on top in laddering hands up the softball bat got to pick first and the loser second and so it went — back and forth — until all the boys who were considered good enough to be on a team had been picked. Then Ernie and Junior laddered the bat again to see which side would get up first and the losing side took to the field to be joined by the little boys who hadn't been picked and us older girls who were allowed to act as sort of permanent supplementary fielders. And for the rest of the week the teams remained locked, at every recess and lunchtime, in one long softball game which had, as we discovered to our surprise several years later when the television came through, some strange rules.

The way we played, for example, every single boy had to get out before the other team could come in. And any boy hitting a home run not only had the right to bat straight away again but also to bring back into the game any boy who had got out. Which led to kids who couldn't remember their six-times table properly being able to announce — say, by noon on Thursday — "The score's now 46 to 39 because, in the last inning starting Tuesday lunchtime, Junior's team was all out except for Irving Snell, who hit three homers in a row off of Lorne Ripley, and brought in Ira and Jim and Elton who brought in the rest except for Austin who got out for the second time on Wednesday with a fall ball one of the girls caught behind third base . . ."

Some days it got so exciting that at noon we couldn't wait to eat our lunches but would rush straight into the schoolyard, gobbling our sandwiches as we ran, toward that aching moment when the ball, snaking across the yellow grass or arching toward us from the marsh sky, might meet our open, eager hands.

So it was a hard blow, Monday morning recess, when Ernie Chapman whirled the bat around his head, slammed it down as hard as he could on home base and announced, "The first girl that goes out to field, *we break her neck.*" We clustered forlornly around the girls' entry door knowing there was nothing we could really do.

"Oh, Alma," mourned Minnie Halliday, biting the ends of her long, brown braids, "why couldn't you just have kept your mouth shut?" It was a bad moment. If we'd tried to go out to field they'd have picked us off one by one. We couldn't even play softball on our own. None of us owned a bat and ball.

If it hadn't been for Doris Pomeroy we might have broken ranks right there and then. Doris, who was in grade 9 and had had a home permanent and sometimes wore nail polish and had even, it was rumored, gone swimming in the quarry all alone with Elton Lawrence, flicked a rock against the schoolhouse wall in the silence following Minnie's remark and steadied us all by saying: "Don't be foolish, Minnie. All we have to do is wait. They need us to field and, besides, they kind of like to have us out there looking at them when they get up to bat."

But it was a long, hard week. Besides not letting us field, the boys picked on us whenever they got the chance. I guess they figured that if they made things bad enough for us, sooner or later we'd go to Miss Ralston and ask her to forget the whole thing. But all their picking on and bullying did was to keep us together. Whenever one of us was tripped going down the aisle or got an ink ball in her hair or got trapped in the outhouse by a bunch of boys it was as if it was happening to all of us. And looking back on that week — when there were so many bad feelings and so many new feelings in the air — it was kind of nice, too, because for the first time us girls found ourselves telling each other our troubles and even our thoughts without worrying about being laughed at. And that was something new at our school.

As for Alma, who kept getting notes thrown on her desk promising her everything from a bloody nose to having her pants pulled down, we stuck to her like burrs. But maybe Alma's hardest moment had nothing to do with bullying at all. It was when her cousin Arnold came over to see her Wednesday after school and asked her to drop the whole idea of girls going for the water.

"If they find out about it, Alma," said Arnold, "they'll probably take away the water bucket."

"Who's they?" asked Alma. She and Arnold had played a lot together when they were little kids and she was used to listening to his opinions on most things.

"Well, the health inspector," said Arnold, "and guys like that."

"They'll never take away that water bucket," said Alma, though she wasn't all that sure. "They don't care who carries the water as long as it gets carried."

"Alma," said Arnold earnestly, "the other guys would kill me if they ever found out I told you this but sometimes carrying the water isn't that much fun. On cold days it's real hard work. You're better off in the warm school."

Alma knew what it cost Arnold to tell her this but she stood firm. "I'm sorry, Arnold," she said, "but I'm used to cold weather. In winter I walk to school the same as you." So Arnold went away.

If Miss Ralston, as the week wore on, noticed anything unusual going on in her school she gave little sign of it. She passed out the usual punishments for ink balls, she intercepted threatening notes and tore them up unread, she looked at Alma's white face, and all she asked about were the principal rivers of Europe. Nor were we surprised.

Nothing in our experience had led us to believe the grown-ups had the slightest inkling — or interest — in what really went on with kids.

Only Doris Pomeroy thought differently. "Miss Ralston looks real mad," said Doris as we trailed in thankfully from Friday morning recess.

"Mad?" a couple of us asked.

"Yeah. Like when she comes out to ring the bell and we're all hanging around the entry door like a lot of scared chickens. She rings that old handbell as if she wished all those yelling boys' heads were under it. Of course they do things differently in River Hibbert. I know for a fact that girls there get to play on softball teams just like the boys."

"On teams? Just like the boys?" But it was all too much for us to take in at that moment, so preoccupied were we with that afternoon's decision on the water. All that long, hard week, it was as if Friday afternoon and Junior Red Cross would never come again. Now that it was almost upon us most of us forgot, in our excitement, at least for the time being, Doris' heady remarks about softball.

So at lunchtime, just as the boys were winding up their week's game ("And real great, eh? Without the girls?" Ernie Chapman was gloating loudly from the pitcher's mound), when Miss Ralston, without her bell, leaped through our clustered huddles at the entry door and headed straight toward the softball field, she took us all completely by surprise. Crunch, crunch, crunch went Miss Ralston's bright red loafers against the cinders and the next thing we knew she'd grabbed the bat from Irving Snell and squinting against the sun, was twirling and lining it before our astonished eyes.

"Come on! Come on!" cried Miss Ralston impatiently to Ernie who stood transfixed before her on the pitcher's mound. "Come on! Come on!" she cried again and she banged the bat against the ground.

"Come on! Come on!" cried Doris Pomeroy and we rushed after her across the cinders.

The first ball Ernie threw was pretty wobbly and Miss Ralston hit it at an angle so that it fell sideways, a fall ball, towards George Fowler's outstretched hands. "Ah-h-h-h-h-h," we moaned from the sidelines and some of us closed our eyes so we wouldn't have to look. But George jumped too eagerly for such an easy ball and it fell right through his fingers and rolled harmlessly along the ground.

Ernie took a lot more time over his second pitch. He was getting over the first shock of finding Miss Ralston opposite him at bat and by this time he was receiving shouts of encouragement from over the field.

"Get her! Get her!" the boys yelled recklessly at Ernie and they all fanned out behind the base.

Ernie took aim slowly. None of us had ever seen the pirouettings of professional pitchers but there was a certain awesome ceremony, nevertheless, as Ernie spat savagely on the ball, glared hard at Miss Ralston, slowly swung back his big right arm and, poised for one long moment, his whole body outstretched, threw the ball as hard as he could toward home base where Miss Ralston waited, her sturdy feet braced against the cinders, her body rocking with the bat.

For a fleeting moment we had a glimpse of what life might be like in River Hibbert and then Miss Ralston hit the ball.

"Ah-h-h-h-h-h," we cried as it rose high in the air, borne by the marsh wind, and flew like a bird against the sun, across the road and out of sight, into the ox pasture on the other side.

"Ah-h-h-h-h-h . . ."

We all stared at Miss Ralston. "School's in," she announced over her shoulder, walking away. Hitting the ball into the ox pasture happened maybe once a year.

That afternoon, toward the end of Red Cross, there was a big hush all over the room.

"Next week," said Miss Ralston, closing the school register, tidying her books, "next week Alma Niles and Joyce Shipley will go for the water."

She swept her hand over the top of her desk and tiny dust motes danced in the slanting sun.

Acknowledgements

"The Old Demon" by Pearl S. Buck. Reprinted by permission of Harold Ober Associates Inc. Copyright © 1939 by Pearl S. Buck. Renewed 1966.

"The Old Man at the Bridge" from *The Short Stories of Ernest Hemingway*. Reprinted by permission of Charles Scribner's Sons. Copyright 1938 Ernest Hemingway; renewal copyright © 1966 Mary Hemingway.

"The Cheat's Remorse" by Morley Callaghan. Reprinted by permission of the author.

"Risk" by Joanna Russ. Reprinted by permission of Curtis Brown, Ltd., 575 Madison Avenue, New York 10022. Copyright © 1975 Mercury Press, Inc.

"The Most Dangerous Game" by Richard Connell. Copyright, 1924 by Richard Connell. Copyright renewed, 1952 by Louise Fox Connell. Reprinted by permission of Brandt & Brandt Literary Agents, Inc.

"The Harps of Heaven" reprinted from *The Long Haul and Other Stories*, by John Durham, copyright 1968, with permission of Webster/McGraw-Hill.

"In the Long Run" by Robert Fontaine. Reprinted by permission of Blassingame, McCauley & Wood, the author's agents.

"The Dentist and the Gas" by Stephen Leacock from *Behind the Beyond*. Reprinted by permission of McClelland and Stewart Limited.

"The Hitch-Hiker" by Gregory Clark. Copyright 1971, Montreal Standard Publishing Company. Reproduced by permission of Optimum Publishing International Inc. from *A Barr'l of Apples*.

"Test" by Theodore L. Thomas. Copyright © 1962 by Mercury Press, Inc. Reprinted from *The Magazine of Fantasy and Science Fiction* by permission of the author.

"The Rocket" by Ray Bradbury. Originally appeared in *Super Science Stories* as "Outcast of the Stars." Copyright 1950 by Ray Bradbury, renewed 1977. Reprinted by permission of the Harold Matson Co., Inc.

"Mariana" by Fritz Leiber. Reprinted by permission of Robert P. Mills, Ltd., the author's agent.

"Annabelle, I Love You" by Mildred Clingerman. Copyright © 1975 by Mercury Press, Inc. Reprinted from *The Magazine of Fantasy and Science Fiction* by permission of the author.

"One Ordinary Day, With Peanuts" by Shirley Jackson, first published in *The Magazine of Fantasy and Fiction*. Copyright © 1955 by Shirley Jackson. Reprinted by permission of Brandt & Brandt Literary Agents, Inc.

"A Man Who Had No Eyes" by MacKinlay Kantor. Copyright © 1931 by Liberty Magazine. Reprinted by permission of Paul R. Reynolds, Inc., the author's agents.

"The Purple Children" by Edith Pargeter. Reprinted by permission of Deborah Owen Limited, the author's agents.

Illustrations

6-7, Co Rentmeester, Life, © Time Inc.
8, 15, 58, 63, 76, Richard Whyte
22, Michael Van Elsen
26, 104, Paul Kaufhold
32, Valerii Shustov
Cover, 34, 53, 80, 99, 118, 148-149, 162-163, 164, 198, Miller Services Limited
39, courtesy Austrian Trade Commission
56-57, The Bettman Archive Inc.
67, courtesy Bulova Watch Company Limited
86-87, from the MGM film, *2001: A Space Odyssey*
88, 145, National Film Board Photothèque
128-129, 130, John Max
110, 170, Michael Semak
137, Jock McRae
189, Richard Erdoes, by permission of Alfred A. Knopf, Inc.

Design by Paul Kaufhold

The publishers have made every effort to trace the source of materials appearing in this book, and would be glad to learn of any errors or omissions in the acknowledgements.